THE BEAST

WALTER DEAN MYERS

Scholastic Press / New York

HENRY COUNTY LIBRARY SYSTEM
COCHRAN PUBLIC LIBRARY
4802 N. HENRY BLVD.
STOCKBRIDGE, GA 30281

HENRY COUNTY LIBRARY SYSTEM
HAMPTON, LOCUST GROVE, McDONOUGH, STOCKBRIDGE

Copyright © 2003 by Walter Dean Myers • All rights reserved. Published by Scholastic Press, a division of Scholastic Inc., *Publishers since 1920*. SCHOLASTIC, SCHOLASTIC PRESS, and associated logos are trademarks and/or registered trademarks of Scholastic Inc. No part of this publication may be reproduced, or stored in a retrieval system, or transmitted in any form or by any means, electronic, mechanical, photocopying, recording, or otherwise, without written permission of the publisher. For information regarding permission, write to Scholastic Inc., Attention: Permissions Department, 557 Broadway, New York, NY 10012.

Gabriela Mistral, "Suavidades" (excerpt) from *Selected Poems of Gabriela Mistral: A Bilingual Edition* (Baltimore: The Johns Hopkins University Press, 1971). Copyright 1925 by Gabriela Mistral. Copyright © 1961, 1964, 1970, 1971 by Doris Dana. Reprinted with permission of Joan Daves Agency/Writer's House, Inc. New York, on behalf of the proprietors.

LIBRARY OF CONGRESS CATALOGING-IN-PUBLICATION DATA
Myers, Walter Dean,
The Beast / by Walter Dean Myers. — 1st ed.   p.   cm.

Summary: A visit to his Harlem neighborhood and the discovery that the girl he loves is using drugs give seventeen-year-old Anthony Witherspoon a new perspective both on his home and on his life at a Connecticut prep school.

[1. Interpersonal relations — Fiction. 2. Schools — Fiction. 3. Drug abuse — Fiction. 4. African Americans — Fiction. 5. Harlem (New York, N.Y.) — Fiction.] I. Title.
PZ7.M992Be 2003   [Fic] — dc21   2002042776

ISBN 0-439-36841-3 (alk. paper)
1 2 3 4 5 6 7 8 9 10
07 06 05 04 03

Printed in the U.S.A.   23 • First edition, October 2003
The text type was set in 11-pt. Sabon • Book design by David A. Caplan

FOR ~~CHRIS~~

For Ava

THE BEAST,

HALF HUMAN, HALF BULL,
ROAMED THE ENDLESS
CORRIDORS OF
THE LABYRINTH,
WAITING FOR THE YOUTH
UPON WHICH
IT WOULD FEED.

— ADAPTED FROM THESEUS AND THE MINOTUAR

PROLOGUE

L*a misma ola vagabunda que te lleva te devuelva.'*
'May the same waters that take you bring you
back to me.' " Gabi kissed my hand twice.

"Are we supposed to make promises to each other
now?" I asked.

"What kind of promises are you going to make to me?"

"I promise to be true to you, and that our first child will
have eyes as dark as the winter sky," I said.

"I'm sure our first child will have dark eyes," Gabi said.
"But I've heard those white girls are easy, so I'm not too

1

sure of how faithful you're going to be. But remember this, a woman can always tell."

"You know what I was thinking?" An old man passed with two small children who were harnessed together. I thought they were probably his grandchildren. "I was thinking that if I get into a good school —"

"Have you heard anything?"

"No, but say I do. I mean, that's the main reason I'm going up to Wallingford, right? Anyway, I was thinking that if I did get accepted at a good school, we wouldn't have to wait until I graduated before we were married."

"How did you figure that?"

"Well, I was reading this piece on the Internet the other day, and they were saying that an Ivy League education is worth a hundred and some thousand dollars a year. So, if I got into one of the Ivies we could get married, borrow the money to live on, and then pay it back later."

"You're sixteen, right?"

"I'll be seventeen in October."

"So two years from now you'll be eighteen."

"You said that people get married at sixteen in the Dominican Republic."

"I said that *girls* get married at sixteen in the Dominican Republic," Gabi said. "And boys if the girl is pregnant."

2

"It'll work," I said.

"It could work," she answered. She bent over my hand and kissed it again. "It could work."

"You nervous about me going?"

"A little," she said.

Gabi leaned back against the bench and put her long legs out in front of her, crossing them at the ankles. She still had her hand on mine. Her hand was the color of golden sand and mine as dark as newly turned earth. That's what she had said on the day we had first admitted to loving one another.

"Do you really think I would start chasing after some blonde just because I was away from the city?" I asked.

"When I was very young, maybe eight or nine, my parents took me to the DR to see some relatives," Gabi said. "In the little town my father was from they had a fortune-teller. She told everyone's fortune and you gave her a dollar.

"When she came to me she said I was very pretty —"

"You're really not that pretty," I said, touching the gentle curve of her cheek. She pushed aside a wisp of wavy hair, then looked up quickly and captured me with eyes so hugely dark and deep that I was once again swimming in the mystery of them. I knew she could sense my heart racing.

"And she said I would always be remembered well.

3

Later, I asked my mother what that meant, and she told me there was a saying that when a man leaves you he'll come back if he remembers you well." Gabi turned her head toward me. "I hope you will remember me well."

"What did you say about the waters taking me away?" I asked.

"May they bring you back to me," Gabi said. "It's from my poet-saint."

"Well, I'll remember where to come and who to come to," I said. "That's my promise to you."

I put my arm around her and Gabi drew close to me. She was small and fit so easily in the curve of my arm. I was nervous about leaving the city, and about the school, but I wasn't concerned with my feelings about Gabi. I knew that I loved her, and that I always would. I don't know how I knew it, but I did.

WALLINGFORD ACADEMY

The rain was beating fiercely against the windows of Hill Dining Hall. A far window was open and the curtains flapped wildly. A dining room worker started toward it. A student, small enough to be a fourth former, beat her to it and closed it. In the corner I saw Brand, his chair tilted away from the round table, his hands clasped behind his neck. Chanelle saw me at the same time and waved me over.

I signaled I would be over in a minute and went for a cup of coffee. An image floated through my mind. My first day at the Academy and Miss Mathews inviting me to have a cup of coffee with her in the dining room. I had never seen a dining room that large before, or floors that nicely cleaned and polished. The sunlight slanting through the windows seemed somehow more subdued than I had ever seen it in Harlem, and the soft lights on the walls and the chandeliers had intimidated me that day and for weeks later.

"The Academy is a place you'll have to get used to," Miss Mathews had said. She had looked closely at me, never mentioning that I was from Harlem, or that her warm tones were meant to suggest a bridge between a black counselor and a black student. I felt good about her. "But the wonderful part of it is that you will get used to it. Students have a way of absorbing the traditions of this school and transforming them into something that resonates with their own lives."

She had been right or, at least, the comfort I began to feel over the next weeks seemed genuine. I noticed that so many of the kids laughed at the idea of tradition, but all of them knew the history of the Academy.

Breakfast had been over for a half hour and the coffee was barely warm in the paper container as I put it down across from Brand. Brand, a face without character, dirty blond hair that would look in place on the six o'clock news in Milwaukee. Chanelle and Julie were sitting with him.

"Here's the deal." Chanelle made her usual parallel hand gestures as she spoke. "Brand is driving down to New York, and so is Julie. Brand has two people going with him and Julie has one, so far. They want us to go but my dad is coming up to take me home and I am absolutely desperate for someone to come with me so I don't have to talk to my father the whole way to New York. So I want you to come with me and my dad."

"I'll be in the city in two hours," Brand said. "Julie is going to crawl in after about two and a half hours. Chanelle's dad is going to take three hours."

"Which is why I need you to come with me!" Chanelle added.

"Okay, I'll go with you," I said.

"What did you think about that math test?" Brand asked.

Chanelle's eyes rolled to the ceiling.

"About halfway through I said a small prayer to the calculus god," I said. "Then I added another one at the end of the test. If I passed it's because one of those prayers got through."

"The problem with your prayers, brother man, is that the calculus god is Asian," Brand said. "He don't want to hear no prayers from no white dudes or no black dudes."

"I think the theory is to give you a math test that's going

to shake you up just before you go on Christmas break," Julie said. "That gives you something to worry about, especially while you wait to hear from your college choice."

The conversation continued about the exams with Brand talking about how the Asians had it made because they were natural test takers and Julie agreeing with everything he said. Julie lived in Fort Lee, New Jersey, just across the George Washington Bridge. She was friends with Chanelle, although I didn't know why Chanelle liked her, and she made sure she kept her distance from me. I was fine with that. I didn't think that Julie wanted to be anywhere near another black person.

There were only a handful of blacks — we called ourselves African Americans at the Academy — in the sixth form. The guys were cool. Some of them thought they were a little special, but I could deal with them. The girls were something else. There were only nine in the sixth and three of them were completely standoffish. The others, except for Julie, were all right but came from a different kind of life than I knew. They were kids, like Chanelle, whose parents had summer homes in Sag Harbor or took them Christmas shopping in London. I thought that maybe one day I would fit in with them, but it would take a while.

Julie, on the other hand, was a trip. She was like an old-time white minstrel dressing up in blackface and woolen wig. Except that under her green eye shadow, auburn wig, and "Oh, my golly!" accent, she *was* black. I told myself that one day I would like to see her naked, no wig, no crazy makeup, no accent, and no exaggerated talk about how she just *loved* baroque music.

We broke up with Brand, actually James Brand, still on a search for riders into the city. Julie took off to gather her laundry to take home.

"You want to walk over to the pond?" Chanelle asked.

The pond. During my first days at the Academy I walked along the path that went around it and tried to ignore it pushing into my consciousness. I made myself think about math and English, and not the differences that Wallingford laid out in this secluded place. Later, as the weather cooled, and the knit pastel scarves and bulky sweaters circled it, I tried not to think of the pond as representing a world I hadn't touched before. It wasn't supposed to feel like home. It was, after all, only water.

"When's your father coming?"

"How much of a hurry are you in?" she asked.

"I haven't been home since I got here in August," I said. We were at the door and I saw that the rain had eased up. There was still a bank of clouds overhead, gray and threatening, but they were moving fairly swiftly toward the west.

"You haven't gone home at all?"

"You know I've been having trouble," I said. "I haven't flunked anything but my grades need all the work I can give them."

She had forgotten I worked in New Haven on weekends. If I could have gotten off from the sneaker store I would have gone home for Thanksgiving, at least.

We started walking across campus. There was still a light rain, but we ignored it. There were cars in the distance, and I imagined that the entire campus would be empty by nightfall. It had been that way at Thanksgiving. I had eaten in the Hall and hung out with some Thai students and the kitchen help until nine. Later I had called home and spoken to Mom and Dad. I didn't get an answer at Gabi's house and that had depressed me. I didn't know if she had received the letter I sent her or not.

"So the truth is" — Chanelle took my arm — "that my father isn't coming, and I bought two tickets for us on the 3:20 Amtrak to Penn Station."

I tried to stop and she pulled me along. Chanelle had been a friend from the time I reached the Academy. Perhaps not so much a friend as the most completely honest person I had met so far at Wallingford. Maybe they were the same thing.

"I was supposed to stay with my dad because I've been doing the switching bit — one holiday with my mom, and one with him — since they've been divorced."

"The courts made that arrangement?"

"No, they were being what they called civilized, only I'm the one who's being split up and I'm the one who has to jump back and forth and understand who's sleeping with who and why it's not really anyone's fault that they're not together," Chanelle said. "I've tried to be understanding of them both and now I'm just tired of it. I'm staying with my mom over the holidays because I feel like it."

"And you want somebody to ride the train with you."

"Spoon, how did you guess?"

"And you blow my chance for a ride without even asking?"

"You don't like Brand, and you don't want to ride all the way down to New York with Julie," Chanelle said. "Case closed. We go over to the chapel, pick up my music, pick up our bags, and then we take the shuttle over to the train station. Right?"

"I guess."

Chanelle was walking next to me, pushing against me even when weren't touching. She was pretty. She moved well, her legs were strong, and sometimes I knew, even when I wasn't around, she thought about me. But I didn't know that.

Chanelle sang hymns and went to the candlelight service on Sunday evenings. It was a simple service, and beautiful. The light in the chapel varied quite a bit. In August, when I first arrived at the Academy, there was an open, warm feeling to the blend of the evening sun and the chapel lights. Later, as the days shortened and the lights dimmed, the flicker of candlelight across the tapestry could lift the spirit and make it soar.

She got her music and showed it to me.

"The music pleases you," I said.

She nodded. Yes, it did.

THE TRAIN TO NEW YORK

I like trains. As opposed to airplanes — there is a sameness about flying, the gray seats in the waiting areas, the identical people checking tickets behind the identical desks. On the plane everyone sits upright, strapped in, facing the same way. The train moves sometimes smoothly, sometimes in fits and jerks. You can feel the curves, the stilted rhythm of the rails. People relax on trains, they sprawl across the seats, some read while others sleep. They face in different directions.

I once took a trip to Savannah with my parents for

Thanksgiving. Two hours into the trip my father was complaining, telling my mother how he would never go by train again. But I loved it. The train was impossibly crowded with people headed south for the holiday. There were suitcases everywhere, not the kind you see on planes — smart, nearly new bags of synthetic fibers — but duffel bags and old suitcases with duct tape holding them together. I imagined these same people, perhaps their parents, coming up from the south thirty years earlier. I knew my father, with his Strivers Row mentality, wouldn't like it, but I did.

"I'll get home by six, and the first thing my mother will want to do is to go out to a fancy grocery store and buy something expensive and barely edible," Chanelle said. "She'll go into her usual shock that I'm still a vegetarian. After that it's the Significant Sit Down where she asks me to tell her all about school. She won't listen to a word, but I'll be up until midnight talking to her."

"It's what parents do," I said. "They have lists in their heads and check off things as you talk. In ten years we'll be doing the same thing."

"You just going to hang out, or do you have plans?"

"I'll have to see what's going on," I said. "Brand said he was going to try to get a game up with some guys he knows. Other than that I don't know."

"What's your girl like?"

What's my girl like? Do I frame Gabi? Do I defend her? Why does my mind race for answers to such a simple question? What is my girl like?

"You'd like her," I finally answered. "She's smart, cool. She wants to be a media specialist on the college level but I think she could make it as a writer."

"If I give a party, do you think she'd come?" Chanelle asked.

"I guess so. Why not? Are you giving a party?"

"I might. I have to do something to keep my sanity."

I'd lost Chanelle's thoughts. Did I ever have them? We sat for twenty minutes in New Haven, changing engines, and Chanelle opened the novel she had brought along. I was thinking about Gabi. At first we had communicated by phone, excited calls with me telling her about the Academy and her telling me how proud she was of me, but how much she missed me. Then her phone had been cut off. I wrote to her and she had answered, a beautiful letter, handwritten, rich with her feelings about what was going on in the neighborhood. She told me that her grandfather, nearly blind, had come to live with them, and that it was a good thing. She apologized for her phone. *"Habla* poverty?" she had asked.

I worked hard on my letter to her, trying to describe what life was like at the Academy, trying to put down on paper what I felt about it. I didn't want to make it seem too good, I knew. The kids weren't any smarter than at our high school in Harlem, but they had already been so many places. Their parents were doctors, or lawyers, or business executives, people who had done all the right things and made the right decisions. Chanelle's father was an editor at a financial newspaper. All the kids, even the ones who complained the most about how phony the Academy was, or how out of touch their parents were, expected to follow the right paths. Or, at least, they knew what paths to follow. What did my homeboys know?

The last letter from Gabi had been at the beginning of December. Overnight Wallingford had been blanketed with almost a foot of clean white snow. Chappie, the ex-army sergeant who worked at the Academy and who had appointed himself keeper of the "boys," gave me the letter along with an overstuffed envelope from the University of Wisconsin. Wisconsin was my second choice of schools after Brown, and I opened that letter first. It said how glad they were that I had applied and told me to fill out the enclosed forms for financial aid. Nothing special, no definite aid, or admission.

What I wanted was for all of my letters to Gabi to be special, to be the kinds of letters someone years in the future would read and wonder about. Even before opening her letter I had imagined my reply, how the snow had fallen in the night and how beautiful the trees around the pond, their bare limbs dressed in the white fluffiness of clean snow, had been in the morning.

Gabi's letter had been long and rambling. She talked about her mother getting on her case and people talking behind her back. There was an oddness in what she was saying, almost an anger. She said that she wished I had made it home for Thanksgiving.

I was sorry I didn't make it home for Thanksgiving. I was sorry that I didn't know why I didn't make it home for Thanksgiving. Was my need to work so compelling? Were the pumpkins in the windows of Wallingford's quaint stores so inviting?

I tried to think about what I would say to Gabi. I called her number and was told the phone was still disconnected. Going down to Harlem would only take a few hours and I could have borrowed the money, but I didn't.

I called Mom and asked her if Gabi had been by, and when she said no I asked if she would go over to her house. She said she would. Later she called me and said that Gabi's mother was ill, and that was probably why I hadn't heard from her.

Gabi had called the next day from a pay phone. She laughed off the letter, saying that I sounded like a soap opera character. She said she had been offered a scholarship to Columbia, and would I consider going there? Yes, of course I would if I could get in, I had said. But Columbia had been a surprise. I hadn't known she had applied.

"Who do you think I should invite to the party?" Chanelle's voice broke through my thoughts. "I don't want it to be just kids from the Academy."

"What kind of party do you want to have?"

"Something that doesn't end in kids puking and crying," she said. "You think a poetry slam would be too corny?"

"Not if you know enough poets," I answered. "You remember the poetry slam they had in the Hall and nobody brought any poems?"

"And Brand dissed the whole thing with his stupid rap? I remember that part," Chanelle said. "I'm just getting depressed going home. Holidays are not my thing. Especially Christmas."

"Why especially Christmas?"

"Because it's here now," she said. "If it was April it would be especially Easter."

The train stopped and two young nuns got on. They were dressed in regular clothes except for their headgear. One of them, very pretty but overweight, smiled at us. I thought of a Guy de Maupassant story in which a nun was hijacked by a robber.

"I could be a nun," Chanelle said. "I don't think it'd be so bad."

"First you live with me for a year on a desert island," I said. "Then you join the nunnery."

"Mr. Witherspoon!" Chanelle put on her *Gone With the Wind* accent. "How you do go on!"

The train started again and the conductor was telling us how many minutes we were from Bridgeport. Chanelle got up to go to the cafe car and asked me if I wanted anything. I said no and she looked at me for a long moment before she left.

The nun who had smiled at me before smiled again and I smiled back.

"Are you on Christmas break?" she asked. "I see your books."

"Yes."

"Us, too," she said.

I hadn't thought of nuns being on Christmas break and it amused me. When Chanelle came back I told her that the nuns were also on Christmas break, and she started talking to them and found out they were both beginning teachers.

Co-op City. The huge, ugly buildings loomed against the gray sky, emphatically announcing CITY.

"You have my number, right?" Chanelle looked up from her book.

"Yes."

"Can I have yours? Is it all right? Maybe we can all have lunch or something? Is that all right?"

"Yeah. Sure."

"No, really, you don't seem too cool with it," Chanelle said.

"I'm cool with it," I said. "You know, I'm just a little nervous."

"Then I won't call." Chanelle shrugged, her hands turned outward.

"No, I don't mean about you calling," I said. "I'm just a little nervous about going home. Is that weird, or what?"

"Why are you nervous?"

I shrugged. As we went into the tunnel leading to Pennsylvania Station I could feel my stomach tense. And suddenly I knew there was a reason I hadn't been home since August. It wasn't exactly clear to me, but I knew it had to do with the mix. Chanelle, Brand, even Julie had all taken the train or driven from New York up to Wallingford, but the distances had been different. They had taken their lives, their successes, with them, and I had left mine behind.

The train stopped at 34th Street, under Madison Square Garden, the home of the New York Knicks. The station was crowded. The escalator up to the main floor. A black man with a paper cup and a toothless grin.

"Can you spare two quarters for a brother?"

"You okay?" Chanelle asked. There was a crowd, moving smoothly through the station, going a hundred different directions, busily weaving the shadowed mosaic of New York. "You're always so laid back and everything. You sure you're okay?"

"I'm okay," I said. "I'll call you."

Chanelle smiled, put her hand on my arm as she kissed me on the cheek, and turned toward the taxi stand.

For a moment I was confused. I told myself that everything was indeed all right.

HARLEM, 356 WEST 122ND STREET

It was New York, my New York, but it felt different. I had only been away a few months but I had already lost the feeling for the crowds, the faster pace. Intending to go straight home, I had taken the A train at 34th. Then I remembered what Chanelle had said about having to explain what I had been doing in school. My parents would expect the same, and I wanted to see Gabi first. I got off the train at 125th and walked down to her block.

The brownstones on 122nd had been converted to two apartments and sometimes more on each floor. Morningside Park was across the wide avenue and gave an airy feel to the block. A wide variety of brown-skinned girls were jumping double Dutch on the sidewalk. Some young boys were sitting on a stoop, a boom box just above them spewing out a rap song. They stared at passersby, daring them to make a comment on either the volume or the string of profanities. I looked to see if Gabi's younger brother, Rafael, was among them; he wasn't.

Gabi's bell was still broken, with the wires coming from the wooden door frame. As I had a hundred times, I took the wires in my hands and touched them together to ring the bell. A moment later I heard the buzzer and pushed open the door. The hallway was musty, and the smells from a mixture of different foods cooking competed in the vestibule.

There were flights up to the top floor and her apartment. The book I had bought Gabi was still in my overnight bag, and I wished I had giftwrapped it even though it was only a used copy of Gabriela Mistral's poems, translated by Langston Hughes. Gabi had been named, by her grandfather, for the Chilean poet.

The door opened. Rafael.

"Yo, what's going on?" Street tough. We touched fists and he moved away from the door.

"So, what's up?"

"The world is still spinning," Rafael said. "And I ain't fell off yet so I must be doing something right."

Rafael was thirteen and smart, but didn't want anyone to know it. He pointed to a chair and told me to "cop a squat" while he went to get Gabi.

The kitchen was small. The shelves were lined with yellow and green placemats that had been cut to fit them. The stove was old enough to look like an antique, and I remembered when Gabi and I had touched up the green enamel and painted the black iron legs. When the gas oven was on full blast it looked like a portable inferno, which came in handy on those winter days when the landlord didn't send up any heat.

"She'll be out in a minute," Rafael said as he came back into the kitchen. He was pulling on his jacket. "I got to go check out my peeps."

"See you around."

Rafael left and I sat alone in the kitchen for a few minutes. Then I heard a door open and heard a man's voice.

"*¿Hola? ¿Gabriela?*"

"Hello," I said, standing as the old man entered the room. "I'm Anthony Witherspoon, Gabriela's friend."

The man stopped in the doorway, as if he were unsure of his bearings. Then he called Gabi's name several times. He held onto the doorframe as he spoke, and I realized he was either blind or couldn't see very well.

A moment later I heard footsteps and Gabi, in a housecoat, her hair combed out and haloed around her head, came into the kitchen. She put her arm around the old man and said something to him in Spanish. He nodded and held out his hand.

I shook his hand. He had a good grip. "You don't speak Spanish?"

"No, I don't," I said. "Gabi's promised to teach me, but she's fallen behind in her lessons."

"Spanish is a beautiful language," the old man said. I figured he was the grandfather who had come to live with them. "Sometimes, near the waterfront, I used to have my tea in the afternoon and listen to the little girls talk as they played. When Spanish is spoken like that it doesn't have to be fancy talk to sound like music."

"That sounds good to me," I said.

"Maybe I'll listen to the radio," he said, putting his hand on the wall, feeling his way out of the kitchen.

As the old man headed toward the bedroom Gabi followed, her hand on his shoulder, smiling back at me. I felt suddenly awkward, too large for my skin, too clumsy to be in her presence. She disappeared down the hallway and a moment later I heard the sound of the radio being tuned to a Spanish-language station.

She came back quickly and put both arms around my waist and squeezed me. "When did you get home?" she asked.

"I haven't been home yet," I said. A hint of perfume, the feathery touch of her hair against my face, the warmth of her body against mine, sent a rush of blood to my head.

As we kissed she ran her fingernails lightly across my chest. "It's so good to see you," she said. "You want tea? Juice?"

"Juice is fine. How are you?"

"Mom is in the hospital," she said, looking into the refrigerator. "Just an overnight thing. She's got a touch of the flu. Some woman she knows told her not to get shots, so she comes down with everything. Plus we've got a little stress with Abuelo living with us."

"You look good," I said. She was wearing an old housecoat, dark brown with a floral design. As she moved from the refrigerator a glimpse of almost golden thigh contrasted with an off-white silk slip. But once again it was the glance, those dark eyes pinning my butterfly heart with a sudden thrust, that recreated the memory of who she was. *You look good.*

"How long will you be home?" She put the juice and a glass on the table.

"Ten days. I'm off all next week," I said. "I had wanted to plan something, but . . . How's your time?"

"With my mother in the hospital and Abuelo living with us I'm running a bit," she said. "But if you're still Spoon, and I'm still Gabi, I have time for you."

"Good. Good." I was searching for words. "How's the writing going? Are you still working around themes?"

"You want to take a walk?" she asked. "I'll get dressed."

"Sure."

She smiled again and went toward her bedroom. From the other room I could hear Abuelo's radio. Strings. A plaintive reed finding a melody and then the same melody repeated in the strings. An image of the old man listening to the music and feeling its colors with his mind. Another image, from Morningside Avenue, the distant silhouette of Riverside Church, the red light at its very top to warn low-flying planes. Why the image? Why not think about Gabi?

Thin. She was thinner. Or was she? Could I have remembered her fuller than she was? She had said that her mother had the flu. Was she also ill?

"Spoon?" Gabi standing in the doorway, the angles of

her body interrupting the rectangle of the door. "I was thinking, maybe I should stay home in case the hospital calls. We can make it a long day tomorrow. Maybe I'll even get up the nerve to read you some of my poems. Have you been writing?"

"No. I've been hitting the books so hard . . ."

"Is the Academy really all that hard?"

"Not really," I said. "But the students there all have a real kick-butt attitude that says they're the best. And I keep telling myself that I don't have anything to prove. You know what I mean?"

"Yes, I think so. You'll tell me all about it in the morning? Come over early and I'll make you breakfast, okay?"

Yes. We agreed upon a time and she kissed me at the door. The kiss was tender, but not eager. I was nervous and thought that she might be, too. How long had I been away?

"Gabi?"

"Yes?"

"Are you still . . . you know?"

She touched my lips with her fingers and nodded yes. Her mouth tightened as she looked up at me and nodded again. "We're still," she said.

In the street I felt good, but slightly wary. It was as if I were looking around a place I hadn't seen before. I passed the girls double Dutching and pretended I was going to jump in and one of them cut me down with a look. The walk from 122nd Street to my folks' place on 145th and Bradhurst was a long one, but I started it.

I thought of Gabi again. She had made me feel good saying that we were still close, but I had felt the need to ask her. Back at the Academy I had thought so many times about touching her again, about slicing through the colors of discovery and settling into some sphere we would both recognize as where we should be now. But I had been hesitant, and it had been Gabi who had put off our being together until tomorrow.

The streets were crowded. Walking along St. Nicholas Avenue I was surprised to see so many people just standing around on the sidewalks, just doing whatever business they had to do, shopping, talking, sitting on folding chairs in front of the small stores. At the Academy we were always conscious of the luxury of sitting in the square or around the pond. It was a good thing to do, to be outside. I sensed a rhythm that my feet felt awkward stumbling through. It was funny. I had been away for only a few months from the place I had spent almost all of my life, and suddenly it was ahead of me, like a shadow on the cracked concrete sidewalk, mimicking my every move.

THE BLOCK — 145TH STREET

The street was incredibly busy and I felt hemmed in as I weaved my way through a sea of people. What I had packed in my memory of Harlem, had taken with me to Wallingford, had been the colors: vibrant Gauguin hues almost bursting from the squared city canvas, barely subdued by the earth tones of people gliding gracefully through the streets. Now there were arrays of the disheveled, eyes dulled from wine or boredom, soft angles against the dark bricks, watching from the stoops as I passed by. Young men, puffed up by bulky jackets, stared from their posts like lions in the high grass watching a passing herd of antelope. I walked faster. Could I remember the cadence of the strut? Could I have forgotten it so soon?

On the corner there was a pile of black plastic garbage bags. Children played around it. The gray metal garbage cans along a railing had eyes painted on them. One of the eyes was winking. Art.

As I approached my stoop I saw Junebug, Ray, and Brian. Brian saw me first and pointed. Not realizing I was tense, I felt myself begin to relax.

"Yo, man, we heard you was in jail!" Junebug put both palms out and I slapped them. "You on parole or you escaped?"

"I'm home for the holidays," I said, sitting next to Ray. "What you guys up to?"

"Ain't nothing going on," Brian said. He looked down the street as if he were looking for somebody. I knew he wasn't. "The biggest thing that happened around here was that Clara got pregnant."

"Clara? You mean light-skinned Clara, live on the Ave?"

"Yep," Ray said. "That's the one. And she's not saying who the baby's daddy is, so you better stay away from her."

"I thought she was supposed to be Miss Perfect," I said.

"I sure didn't expect to see her on the sports pages," Junebug said.

"You see my man Scott around?" I asked.

"Yeah, he's going to art school at night. Downtown somewhere," Brian said. "You play any ball up in that school you going to?"

"A little," I said. "I'm working part time."

"My father said if you get into a prep school you can get a scholarship easy," Ray said. "I was thinking about going to one of those schools, but I don't think I could deal with all the rules and stuff."

"They got a lot of rules?" Brian asked.

"Not really," I said, standing up. "Let me go on upstairs and check out the folks. I'll catch up with you guys later."

"You can catch up with me and Junebug," Ray said, a broad grin across his face. "Don't hang out with Brian because he's one of them bad elements the parole officers keep talking about."

"Man, get out of here." Brian narrowed his already narrow eyes even farther and Ray played it off with a grin.

I had known all of them, Ray, Junebug, and Brian, for years. The day I had left they had been sitting on the stoop. I started into the hall and had almost reached the elevator when I heard somebody coming up behind me. I turned and saw Brian. He had gotten taller, at least six two, maybe six three.

"Yo, man, I just want to tell you something," he said. "You know Rafe, right?"

"Yeah, Gabi's brother."

"I heard he was gang banging right after Halloween," Brian said. "It probably don't mean nothing, but I just thought I'd pull your coat."

"Gang banging? Rafe? Yeah, thanks."

Brian and I exchanged high fives and I got into the elevator. Was it smaller than it had been? Were the light brown metal walls more depressing?

Fourth floor. My thoughts jumbled into each other. I needed to see my parents, to re-connect with them and, at the same time, make sense of what Brian had said. What was Rafe doing trying to get into a gang? Somehow the world seemed to be spinning in a different direction.

The door opened. A brown-skinned man, glasses halfway down his nose. He turned and called into the apartment.

"Eloyce! It's a guy selling encyclopedias. You want any?"

"No, we've got one on the computer," my mother answered.

My father pulled me into the apartment and hugged me and suddenly I felt like crying I was so glad. We went into the living room. The evening news was on and Mom turned from it when we entered the room.

"Oh, baby!" She jumped up and ran to me. More hugs, more kisses. It was so good to be home and I let the warmth of it rush over me.

"So, say something smart!" my dad said. "All the time you've been gone you should know everything."

"How are you doing up there?" Mom asked.

"I'm doing all right," I said, flopping down onto my old seat on the right side of the couch. "We're going through the college square dance now. I told you I applied to Brown and a few other colleges, right?"

"You should think some more about accounting," my father said, nodding in agreement with himself. "You got the qualifications to be a certified public accountant. You get your certification and you got a job for life."

"If you don't love accounting you shouldn't get into it," Mom countered, riding her mom's horse to the rescue. "Anthony has to make up his own mind and find something he truly loves."

"I'm not telling him what to do, Eloyce," Dad said defensively. "But he should know his options. When I was his age I didn't know a thing about a job. If I had I might have been a lawyer or something."

"Is that what you wanted to be?" I asked. "A lawyer?"

"No, what he wanted to be was an explorer," Mom

said. "You know, Matt Henson lived right up the street in the Dunbar Apartments and that's what he wanted to do. Run off to the North Pole or something like that. Isn't that right?"

"You just can't get into the exploring business," my father said, settling into his chair. "Anyway, there's a difference between something like that and a real job. When he finished exploring, Matt Henson worked for the government, same as I do."

The conversation was a net, loosely thrown out to gather the nostalgic moments we tossed into the middle of the room. They kidded me with a hundred questions. Mom had asked them all on the phone, but now she sat in front of me, her hands in her lap, and looked at me as I answered. I wanted to ask her if I'd changed. She hadn't. She was still pretty, still younger than the age on her driver's license. In her voice there was still the faint lilt of Saint Kitts. I still thought my father had been lucky to find her before she realized how beautiful she was.

"The thing I had to learn," I said, "was that the kids who do well study all the time, not just when they take tests. It's like a habit for them. Once I got that into my head I could deal with the academics. I also found out that some of the kids who didn't study were being passed anyway because nobody wanted them to flunk out. That's the dark side of the Academy. They need to make everybody look smart."

"You have to study," my father said. "That was the last thing I said to you before you left for school."

"That's right," I answered.

It's what I was supposed to do, to tell him that I understood the wisdom he offered, and I did.

There were four small porcelain elephants on the upright piano. The first one was slightly larger than the others, and they graduated in size until the smallest one, barely an inch high. On the mantle there were porcelain dogs and cats. They were so familiar, I had counted them a hundred times and knew that, around the room, there were twenty-seven porcelain animals. But now I saw them.

Dad had had a few beers and dozed off in his chair. Mom got him up and, after another hug for me, he was shuttled contentedly off to the bedroom. She came back and asked me if I was tired.

"You trying to put me to bed?"

"I'd like to see you snuggled safe and sound in your own bed," she said, revisiting Momtalk. "Yes."

"I stopped by Gabi's house on the way home," I said.

"Her mother's very sick," Mom said, folding her hands in her lap. "I don't think her family is doing well."

"Oh?" I was disappointed that I hadn't sensed that Gabi's mother was so ill. "I didn't know that."

"I know Gabi's very special to you," Mom said. "When somebody is so special you don't always listen closely enough to what they're saying."

Mom tiptoed over and rubbed her nose against the underside of my chin.

"A man's stubble," I said, using my most manly voice.

"Poof!" she answered.

In the darkness of my room I replayed my homecoming. Five months was not that long, but it was long enough to shift perspective, I thought, to discover new shadings and to question old ones.

I thought about the 'hood. In the morning it would fall into place again, jumping with life, with brightness, alive.

My parents were the same, and not the same. My mother, so sweet, was still the safe haven against any storm. But now I saw her as the dark and gentle guardian angel that she was. My father's rituals, his search for the proper things to say, him reminding me that I needed to think about making a living, had moved beyond the annoyance I used to feel into a kind of comfort zone.

The stone steady stoop was the same. The guys had laughed about Clara being pregnant. It was really sad, and they all knew it. In a way they were all disappointed, but sadness doesn't wear well in the 'hood, and so they had thrown it out as if it didn't matter. As if nothing was so serious that it couldn't be laughed off. But Brian hadn't thrown away what he knew about Rafe.

And here was Anthony Witherspoon, the big Spoon, the great observer.

"Mr. Witherspoon, do you find yourself amusing?" a math teacher at the Academy had asked when I had missed an easy problem.

Sometimes I did. Yes.

TAR BEACH

You want me to come up with you?" Rafe had asked.

"No," Gabi had said.

Gabi and I had taken a folding table to the roof. There were already two milk crates up there and Rafe realized we were going to have breakfast. It was so much like Gabi, finding private moments on top of the world. Someone had rigged up an electrical connection and she plugged in the hot plate.

"How do you want your eggs, kind sir?"

"Sunny-side up," I said.

Gabi's roof overlooked 122nd Street in front, and a patchwork of yards in the back. The yards, some with trees, others with clotheslines, were marked off by fences. A black cat crept along one of the fences and stopped when a dog, it looked like a pit bull, strained forward, barking. The cat stayed frozen for a few seconds, then realizing that the dog was not able to reach him, walked slowly the rest of the way into the next yard.

"My mother's really sicker than I thought." Gabi sat at the table, her coat open, her wide dress tucked between her legs. "I called the hospital this morning and the doctor said her infection flared up again."

"How sick is she?"

"It comes and goes. They found a few cancer cells in her stomach lining and she's been taking chemo just as a precaution. Sometimes it doesn't look so bad, sometimes it does. It's just when she gets home she gets depressed," Gabi said. "It's depression on top of the illness. So she's cramping up and crying for God to help her and then she's saying that she'll be glad when it's over. I keep telling her that if she takes care of herself physically she'll feel better inside. Last week she called my father and asked him to come back. Can you imagine that?"

"He's married again, right?"

"And she knows that," Gabi said.

She was eating bread and strawberry preserves and there was a crumb on her cheek. I took it off and touched her lips with my fingers.

"Is he okay?" I asked. "Your father?"

"Her life is getting to be like a huge puzzle." Gabi went on about her mother, ignoring my question. "She goes to church three times a week, she lights candles, she goes to a woman who reads her tea leaves, everything. I started a poem about her, I wanted to call it 'Black Clouds,' but then I switched it to 'Nubian Clouds' and it became a poem about black warriors. Isn't that stupid?"

"You think she's going to make it?" I asked. "Is the chemotherapy working?"

"The doctors say that she'll be okay if she's strong." Gabi closed her eyes and tilted her head back. "I don't really know, but sometimes I think she has too many paths in her life."

"Maybe it's good her father came to live with you," I said.

"Do you know how easy it is not to be strong?" she asked, suddenly opening her eyes. "Sometimes she says she wants to give her life to God. But when those words come from her mouth I only hear 'giving your life.' I know she's thinking about her life in the DR, and that has a meaning to her that I don't even know about. She's faithful to my father even though he's moved on with his life. She even lights candles for him. She thinks she's led a good life, like a *campesina*, a peasant woman, and all she wants is for God to tell her what to do.

"She's not that complicated a person when you get right down to it, and all of this, when you add the sickness to it, is like some giant labyrinth that she's stumbled into. She takes a step and then pulls her foot back. Whatever path she takes makes her worried about the ones she didn't."

"That's got to be a downer."

"Maybe. But she has to do something. There's no use in feeling sorry for yourself. You live, you have choices, and you have to make them."

The eggs, sunny-side up with onions and salsa, were good. Gabi tried to make tea but the hot plate wouldn't get hot enough to bring the water to a boil. I asked Gabi if she had made up her mind about Columbia and she shook her head no.

"It was more talk than anything real," she said. "The guidance counselor is telling me — what did he say? — that if I apply I'm sure to get it, and I'm thinking that it's like the lottery, a dollar and a dream, only what are your chances? You know what I mean?"

I knew what the words meant. I didn't know why she turned away as she spoke, or why her voice cracked.

"I'm checking the mail, waiting to see what offers are out there," I said. "But I think going to the Academy might un-blacken me to the point where I don't get an offer."

"What are the girls like up there?" She was smiling now, but her eyes had reddened.

"How would I know? All I do is study."

"That's not all you did when you were in Harlem," Gabi said. "And you haven't said anything about missing me so I guess you've found somebody new."

In the street below a fire engine, its horns blasting, passed. I looked around to see if anyone could see us if we kissed on the roof, and figured no one would.

"You know, I was thinking what I would say to you when I saw you," I said. "I had lined up all my 'I love yous' and was even trying to figure out a way to use 'darling' in a sentence. Nobody ever really says 'darling' in real life."

"¡Mi querido!"

"It doesn't count in Spanish."

"So why haven't you said it in English?" She looked at

me intensely, as if she were trying to find a truth in my face.

"I feel shy about it," I said. "We haven't talked much in the last couple of months. It's almost as if we have to get the beat going again. The night before coming back to the city I thought about what we would say, what we would do. I thought about kissing you. Holding you."

"Now I'm the one feeling shy."

"Maybe we should have this huge kissing and hugging session and get a lot of momentum going and see where it leads," I said.

"Let's take it slow, Mr. Anthony Witherspoon," Gabi said. "You can have one kiss today, two tomorrow, and we'll see where that leads. We'll use a quota system. Then we won't be rushing into anything we're going to regret."

"So do you have the urge to throw some 'I love yous' my way?"

"Before you left I thought that you were the most special guy in the whole world." Gabi turned to me, her hands between her legs, her head slightly to one side. "I still feel that way. But when you left and things got really hard here — my mother, my grandfather living with us — life took a little turn. I'm even surer how I feel about you, maybe a little less sure about how I feel about myself."

"When do I get the kiss?"

She smiled, and stood up. "Now, because I have to go downtown to do some business for my mother."

"I'll go with you."

"No."

"Why?"

"It's personal."

"I don't care."

"I do."

She shut off my objections with her hand across my lips. Then, moving her face close to mine, she pulled her hand slowly away. An embarrassing rush of lust swept over me as I felt her tongue slip into my mouth.

We parted and I felt myself trying to catch my breath. "Will I see you later?"

"It depends on my mother," she said. She was stacking the dishes in the center of the card table. "Sometimes she's not too rational. I don't always want to do what she asks me, but she's my mother."

We took the table and dishes down to her apartment. I wanted to kiss her again, and told her. She said no, that she wanted something to look forward to.

"I'll call you tonight, if Mom is okay," she said. "About seven?"

"How's Rafe doing?"

"He's real good," she answered. "He runs the streets a lot, but he's not really getting into anything too heavy. He helps out in the house, too. I'm really proud of him. He just doesn't have that macho thing going on."

I didn't want to go home. I wanted to hang with Gabi and do things for her mother. I wanted to climb her and swim her and find the words she did to say how I felt. I wanted another language to speak to her, to say all the things I was too shy to say in English. I wondered if I would make love to her before I went back to school.

I hadn't wanted to press Gabi about Rafe hanging with a gang. She seemed definite about him being cool and I wondered about it. When I got back home the apartment was empty. My parents were at work and I got out my texts to study. That lasted a minute and I put them away and looked up Brian's number in my address book. He answered the phone and I told him that Gabi had said that Rafe wasn't in a gang.

"I don't know if he's in it or not." Brian's voice sounded nasal on the phone. "But I know he was walking with some bangers."

Lying across the bed, staring up at the ceiling, I felt numb. I told myself that I would speak to Gabi about what

Brian had said. Brian wouldn't like me putting his name in the street, but I decided I would.

The phone rang. Chanelle.

"Come over for pizza tomorrow. Just a few people, mostly kids from the Academy. Bring your girl. Anytime after six, okay?"

Gabi called from a pay phone and I told her about going over to Chanelle's. She said it sounded like fun, that she would love to go.

"I want to check out the Anglo competition," she said.

"It was really good seeing you today," I said. "I especially dug having breakfast on the roof. It was like our little romantic balcony overlooking the Danube, or whatever river they have in the latest James Bond flick."

"Yeah, you've still got it going on," she said. She sounded tired. "I like cooking for you."

"You sound tired. How did it go today? You were doing something for your mother?"

She said it had gone all right, something to do with the Department of Welfare, but that it had been tiring. "And now I have to fix my grandfather's dinner," she said.

I asked if I should call her back later, and she said no, that she would call me in the morning.

"Where are you now?" I asked. I could hear trucks passing by in the background.

"On the way home," she said. "I'll see you tomorrow. Come to my house and we can go to the pizza thing together."

She was off the phone and I felt the distance between us.

Was it Einstein who said that time can be thought of as a fourth dimension? I had been in Wallingford for about five months and now, back in Harlem, the physical dimensions were all the same, the angles still set at the right pitch, the distances still true, but there was change. What bothered me most was that I thought Gabi might be seeing somebody else.

I7 WEST 54TH STREET

New York at night has the illusion of magic, but it is shallow, like the oyster's suggestion of mystery. There is no magic, only the hard shell and the promise of a pearl that is never realized. But even the illusion has resonance in the timid heart and I fought against it as I turned down Fifth Avenue onto Chanelle's block.

Where is the character? I asked myself. How do you grow up in this asphalt cocoon? I imagined Chanelle being taken from one event to another, never once wondering what she would see when she left the house, never questioning if the event would be on time or if she would be well received. I was being condescending. Dee-fense! Dee-fense!

The doorman stood in front of me, his large body blocking the entrance, trying to look intimidating.

"What do you want?" he asked. There was no respect in his voice. The servant assuming the airs of his master.

"Chanelle Burnitz," I said.

"So what do you *want*?" he repeated. He had become derisive. A derision that bordered on the defensive.

I was already mad because Gabi wasn't coming, so the anger bubbled up easily. "Hey, man, she expects me," I said. "So why don't you just do what you need to do and let her know I'm here."

Expected. He looked at me, wondering how to regain the upper hand. We stared at each other for a long moment, both needing a win. He knew that I could not possibly live in the building he was hired to guard. He turned away and picked up the phone. I looked away as he dialed Chanelle's number. Could he possibly have known how he had defeated me?

The elevator. The lackey had already pressed the button for the seventeenth floor. He was telling me that he didn't trust me not to press another button, to hop off the elevator at a floor at which I was not expected and molest the rich white people. Did he know how he had defeated me?

Chanelle's apartment was light, airy. The living room walls were a bland gold, outlined by an equally bland white trim. The furniture was plain, with clean straight lines. The polished walnut table along one wall reflected the small chandelier. The room was nothing until the eye caught the three enormous round windows with their wrought iron and wood design. They were what the room was all about. After the statement of the windows, everything else was just gesture.

I did my counting thing. Me and Chanelle, eleven whites, and an Indian-looking girl in the living room. On a side table there were soft drinks, beer, and what looked like white wine. Chanelle kissed me on the cheek and said she was glad that I'd come. I recognized several faces from Wallingford. There was James Brand, pushing himself into the center of every conversation. Amy Martinson, tall, perfect teeth, perfect moves, perfect casualness. And Chanelle. She was wearing a brown sari. It wrapped around her body, silky and sensuous, and I imagined its coolness against her skin. I tried to think of something else before I fell over.

"So, you down for some ball tomorrow?" Brand asked me.

"Sure, I guess. Where and who?"

"Some brothers from the Drive," he said. "I think three of them played in some church league this year."

"They don't play out of Riverside Church, do they?" I asked.

"What's the difference?" Brand's smile is a practiced crooked.

The difference, I said to myself, is the difference between a great basketball program like the Gauchos and some pickup team. Brand doesn't know basketball in Harlem. He doesn't have to know it, either.

We made arrangements.

There was music from a smoking system. I danced self-consciously with girls dancing self-consciously with me. Chanelle avoided me. She didn't ask me why Gabi hadn't come.

"I'm really stressed out," Gabi had said. "I think I'm coming down with something. Maybe mono, I don't know. Drop by afterward if you want. Can you forgive me this time?"

"Sure," I'd answered.

There had been a time when her kisses had been wolf-hungry, her body eager to push against mine. She would have wanted to see me, to talk to me, to spin out our dreams. Now I was jealous of whoever or whatever had her time and the feeling made me stiff, awkward.

Can you forgive me this time?

The glasses tinkled and the guys hovered until they came to the collective conclusion that they had not discovered anything magical about Chanelle's party, that the girls were not going to be steered into empty bedrooms, and no one was going to have an adventure to talk about for months, or even weeks, to come.

I spent the hours shifting from foot to foot. It wasn't just the white doorman downstairs that made me feel out of place, it was the world that had white doormen and sixteen- and seventeen-year-olds who wore expensive jewelry and dresses that cost as much as some people uptown made in a week. I could dance as well as anyone at the party, even better. But I still felt as if I didn't belong.

"Your girl didn't want to come?" Chanelle finally asked. I was leaning against the wall. Amy and another girl were in the bathroom, and both were crying. I imagined one of them had just lost a lover or an earring. Chanelle put her hand on my forearm and was telling me good-bye.

"We could be drifting," I said. "I don't know."

"So what are you going to do?"

"Well, if I could find a volcano, I could throw myself into it and then she'd be sorry," I said. "Naturally, I'd leave a note. Haiku."

"Do you think she was uptight with the party being down here?"

I shrugged and wondered why I had always thought that the differences were only viewed from bottom to top. Chanelle leaned against me and rubbed my chest with the flat of her hand.

"You're a good guy, Spoon," she said. "You have to keep that in mind."

The elevator again. I was mad at myself for not staying longer, for not making a play for Chanelle.

Why? Why not? What else did I have going on?

You have Gabi, and you love her.

I took the downtown E train at Fifth Avenue and 53rd Street to 42nd Street. Then the uptown A to 125th, and to Gabi's house.

The streets were quiet, dark. There were Christmas lights in the store windows, a huge wreath in the apartment complex on 124th Street. A radio played "Jingle Bells" in Spanish and that lifted me. I rang Gabi's bell and there was no answer. After a second ring someone pulled back the curtain on the vestibule door. It was Rafe.

"Yo, man, it's late."

"I know," I said. "I have to see Gabi."

He didn't answer as he let me in. On the way up he said she was sleeping. I thought I'd made a mistake, that maybe I should leave and come back in the morning. But Rafe was moving faster than I could muster my casual air and so I followed him up.

In the apartment Rafe sleepily pointed me toward Gabi's room. Everything I thought of that was romantic was also corny. I thought of calling her name, kissing her lightly before she was fully awake, then leaving so it would only be a partial memory that would bother her forever. I didn't.

On her dresser was a small plaster statue of the Virgin Mary. There was a candle in front of it and, next to the candle, the reflected light iridescent on its narrow shaft, was a hypodermic needle.

I froze. My heart pounded in my chest. I turned toward where Gabi lay in the middle of the bed, the sheets twisted around and through her brown legs. I called her name.

"Gabi?"

She murmured and reached out her hand. I took it and sat by her on the bed.

"How you doing?" I asked.

"Spoon." Eyes still closed, she put my hand against

her cheek, then, turning, kissed my fingers. "What time is it?"

"Late," I said. "I shouldn't have come by so late."

She pulled the sheet up in front of her. "You shouldn't be seeing me half-naked," she said.

Her shoulder was bare, and I kissed it. We said each other's names at the same time and both smiled.

"How was the pizza party?"

"There's a needle on your dresser," I whispered to her. "Why is there a needle on your dresser?"

One brown leg over the side of the bed. Her foot touched the floor and she lifted herself to see the needle. She sat back down heavily, her head drooped forward. Seconds passed. Perhaps minutes. From the street below her window the constant hiss of cars energized the night.

She lifted her head and pushed her hair away from her face. I could only see the outline of her cheek and the candlelight reflected in her eyes. "Spoon, I'm only skin surfing. Really! Oh God!"

She buried her face in her hands and began to sob. Skin surfing. The words were heavy and dragged me down hard. The vocabulary of drugs was familiar to me. I imagined her "skin surfing," sliding the needle beneath the soft brownness of her skin. Where did she put it? In her thigh? Her arm? It was all violation. A needle sliding between skin and muscle, between trust and despair.

Nearly still in the darkness, her sighs marked the passage of time. I looked at the dresser, the sad Virgin. The flickering candlelight. Our moments were strung together, futile, despairing, like the continued silence between heartbeats.

"Gabi, what can I do? How can I help?"

" '*En una pura noche se hizo mi luto . . .*' "

"Don't go Spanish on me!" I said. "Don't!"

" 'In one pure night my mourning shaped in the labyrinth of my body,' " she said. "Spoon, I have to go to Spanish, or to poetry. I can't stay in this awful place!"

"Gabi, what can I do?"

"Go home," she said. "Think about me. If you can talk to me in the morning, it'll be enough."

Her eyes were half shut, her words slurred. She turned away from me and pulled the sheet over her head.

As I walked into the Harlem night the signs of Christmas were all around me. There was an excitement in the air that was available in even the meanest street. But somewhere, Herod was killing babies.

HARLEM HOSPITAL

I called Gabi in the morning, but the phone was still not working. I spent the day with my mother. We were polite to one another when I knew she wanted warmth. Once, she asked me what I was thinking about, and I couldn't bring myself to tell her.

As we shopped for food my mind raced through one scenario after another. It was my whole life on fast-forward. There was a scene in which I lectured Gabi before I strode triumphantly away. There was a scene in which I took Gabi back to Wallingford with me, and we were reading quietly at the edge of the pond. There was a scene in which I was sitting at her feet, my head resting on her knee as I told her how much I loved her.

But loving her was different now. It was no longer something that could be done from long distance. It had to be the here and now, the immediate. I suddenly understood the words of the marriage ceremony. Do you take this woman? But it is more than that. Do you take this life, these hard streets, or do you run back to Wallingford and tell yourself that the miles between there and Harlem will always protect you?

I was desperate to talk with Gabi again, but I had to spend some time with my parents. I tried to be casual as I kidded with my father, but he knew I was watching the clock and asked me if I was going out. I told him I was thinking about it. Whenever the phone rang I thought it might be her. The smell of frying onions had filled the house, and on the television tiger kittens were being pushed around a sty by a pig when my father called my name.

"Gabi's on the phone," he said, watching for my reaction.

I smiled weakly.

The first thing she said was that Nestor had been stabbed. She asked if I could meet her at the hospital. I said I could, in fifteen minutes. Mom wanted me to eat something before I went. She had already dished it up.

"Will you put it in the refrigerator for me?" I asked.

Of course. I kissed her and started to leave. Dad called me aside and asked if I had any money. I didn't and he gave me twenty dollars. Then he asked me if Gabi was pregnant.

"Not by me," I said, smiling so that he knew it was a joke.

He was upset, and it wasn't fair of me to leave without telling him more. But what would I have said? That Gabi had touched the Black Plague?

Nestor. I remembered a skinny, sallow kid, a friend of a friend, who played clarinet in the school band and later with a Latino group in Elmhurst. Gabi had treated him like a little brother and had tried to get him to write raps in Spanish for the school newspaper.

The hospital emergency room was filled with Saturday-night people. Vine-thin children struggling to breathe through their asthma-congested lungs. An old woman in her nightgown with a swollen face. I heard her say that her daughter had punched her. Her mouth was bleeding. On a small table in one corner stood a pathetic little Christmas tree, its lights blinking on and off, the little brown angel on top leaning to one side.

A nurse looked around the room, trying to pick out the worst cases. She saw a pudgy kid with his foot wrapped in a towel. She touched his foot and he winced in pain. She carefully moved the towel, looked at the foot, announced aloud that the foot was broken, and told him he'd have to wait. There were worse cases.

The kid was pleased.

Gabi came in with Nestor. It was the Nestor I remembered, bent over at the waist. There was an incredibly ugly bloodstain on the front of his chino pants. Gabi was talking to a male nurse as I walked over to them.

"What happened to him?" The nurse was big, thick. He lifted Nestor's head and looked into his eyes.

"He was stabbed," Gabi said. "He can't walk any farther. You have to get a gurney for him."

The male nurse walked away, stopped at a desk, and picked up the coffee container he had left there. No, he didn't have to do anything, he was saying. Life was that cheap.

Gabi looked around for someone else to talk to. She saw a prim woman sitting behind the desk and, leaving Nestor leaning against a pole, went to talk to her. The woman handed her a clipboard with a form to fill out and turned away. I looked at the male nurse and thought he was smirking. I walked over to him.

"Excuse me, I wonder if you can give my friend a hand," I said. "He's really hurt badly."

Satisfied, he said he would see what he could do.

He pulled a gurney from against the wall and wheeled it over to Nestor. I helped Nestor up on it.

"Yo, Spoon." Nestor made a fist and I hit it lightly. "Gabi said you were back, man. Glad to see you, bro."

"Glad to see you, man."

The nurse wheeled him down the hall. Gabi followed them. I didn't know what to do, and so I looked around for a place to sit.

"If he walked in on his own two feet he ain't going to die." This bit of wisdom from a man my height, but heavier than me, maybe two hundred pounds. "When they come in like that it means they haven't lost so much blood they're going to pass out. Then they can patch you up.

"The way he bent over — you see the way he was bent over?"

"Yeah?"

"They got him in the stomach. You get some blood in the stomach, some bleeding and whatnot, but they'll find that."

"Oh, good."

"I bet you're wondering what happened to me, right?"

"Yeah." No.

He pulled his hand from his side and I saw that it was

bandaged heavily. Slowly, like a striptease artist, he started unwinding the gauze. When he got to the end I saw that he'd cut off the tip of his finger, and the last of the gauze was stuck to the bloody stump.

"They'll put some antibiotic on it, put in four or six stitches — they always put in an even amount so they know they don't miss none when they take them out — and I'll be out of here," he said, rewrapping the finger.

Wonderful.

Gabi came out and said that Nestor was taken to X-ray, and that they were going to keep him overnight.

"I'll come back later to see if he's okay. I want to tell his mother."

"How come she doesn't know already?"

"Because she lives in the Bronx and nobody has told her," Gabi said, her voice edged with a sudden annoyance. "When he was hurt he came by my house looking for Rafe. I saw the blood and knew I had to get him here. Help doesn't grow on trees around here, not even Christmas trees. I figured you would help if I needed moral support, and I know we needed to talk."

"You want to go for coffee across the street?"

She said yes and we walked across 135th to the diner. It was fairly crowded, with packages and shopping bags between the seats. Gabi ordered black coffee and I ordered a hamburger.

"So, what do you want me to say?" Gabi looked at me and then quickly away. "You want me to say that I'm mad at myself for using drugs? Say that I know it's all wrong? What do you want me to say?"

"I don't know what I want," I answered. "On one hand I'm thinking speeches, and on the other hand I'm feeling hurt. You're talking as if I'm coming down on you and the real deal is I'm just put out to dry. The woman I love is using. Wow! It's almost too heavy to deal with. What would you say if I told you I was on drugs?"

"I'd say, 'Get off.'"

"Hey, man!" a customer at the counter yelled toward the small clerk at the register. "This sausage ain't even done! I ain't paying for this crap!"

"Free," the man responded, a toothpick dangling from his lips. "You can just walk into Harlem Hospital for free. You don't need no pass or no wounds or nothing. Just tell them you want to be in there for a while."

"I'm talking about these damned sausages, man!"

"I'm talking about this damned shotgun, boy."

He lifted the shotgun from behind the counter, held it up for a few seconds, and put it down again. The customer went through his pockets, found the money for his meal, and left complaining that he would never be back again.

"I spent all day thinking about last night," I said. "It's like something sneaked into my life when I wasn't around."

"The only thing I can say right now is that I'm not a street person." Gabi's lips quivered and she looked away a second, and then back to me. There were tears again. "I always thought I was stronger than the streets."

I didn't know how to answer.

The hamburger came. Tasteless, on a dry white bun, surrounded by soggy iceberg lettuce and a pale tomato. I told Gabi that it was horrible, and she smiled.

I finished half of the hamburger. Gabi finished her coffee and said that she was going back to the hospital. I paid the bill and we went across the street. I sat outside on the bench while she walked down the corridor looking for someone who could tell her about Nestor.

Three white cops came in with a man in handcuffs. There was a knot on the side of his head and blood all down the front of the white shirt he wore. He was cursing and spitting at the cops and anyone he caught looking in his direction. One of the cops, the beefiest, announced that it was a "nut case."

A pretty girl with sweet, pouting lips told the deranged

man that if he spit on her she would cut his heart out because she "didn't play."

The hospital security guard pointed to the clock and mentioned that it was only a quarter past nine. The cops and the guard laughed.

Where was the world I had left behind? What had happened to it? Had something changed, something that wasn't in the papers, that wasn't on television? Or was it me? Had I changed?

Gabi came back. She said that a nurse told her that Nestor was going to be all right and that she had got his mother's number. We went into the other waiting room and Gabi called her.

"Where's your mom?" I asked Gabi as we walked out into the cold December air.

"Downtown," she said. "I spoke to her today."

I took her thin hand in mine. We walked slowly down Lenox Avenue. On 130th Street there were street vendors selling knit hats and T-shirts. Other pushcart people, cooking on makeshift grills, filled the sidewalks with the scents of sausages, onions, and sweet potatoes. When we reached 125th Street we turned and started crosstown to the West Side.

"When I was young my mother said that she used to

love this street because of all the nice things in the store windows," Gabi said. "She said she would give herself an imaginary budget of $100 and pick out things she would buy if she really had the money."

"I've done that," I said. "But that's a long time ago, a different reality."

"And you want to know what's real now, right? Well, what's real is that there are places for everything," she said. "School was in one place, and college applications sat over there, and my mother was over there, and my father and my grandfather were in their places. And you were there, too. Old, shiny, and handsome Spoon, with your nice muscles and your good ears that liked my poems.

"And there was this road through it all, and I could see it." She sighed heavily. "Do you know what I mean?"

"A road?"

"Like you know all of those things are in your life, and you know you need to make sense of them somehow. Then one day you get up in the morning and begin your walk, you say now you need to look at the road, to see how you should move on. And then the road is gone.

"One day . . . no, not one day. One week perhaps, maybe one month, I don't know, it just all stopped being clear. And when it wasn't clear anymore I stopped knowing what was real and what wasn't. The road suddenly became a maze of twisting, winding paths going nowhere. My mother talked to me about leaving school and taking care of Rafael. Abuelo came to live with us. From 'doing all right' we had slipped down to 'just holding on.' I didn't know what to do. What I had been good at doing was thinking, and now I didn't know how to think anymore. All I knew was that I didn't want my life to be my life. I wanted to have somebody else's life. Can you understand that?"

"I want to," I said. "But I can't." We had reached her stoop and sat on it. "I don't understand how you can know something one day and not know it the next day."

"It doesn't make a lot of sense, sometimes, but that's the way it seems when I sit down and try to sort it out myself. I even thought about you and everything you were doing," Gabi went on. "When we were saying good-bye you were so clear. You had plans and places to go and things to do. I think there's a time when we want to think that we all have plans and places to go, and sometimes we really don't."

"Like boys who say they're going to play in the NBA?"

"Or like girls who think they're going to college," she said.

"You don't start using drugs . . ."

"When you know so much?"

"Yeah, that's right," I said. "When you see it all around you and know what it's really like."

"If you see the Beast, you run away," she said. "I didn't run fast enough."

No. No. It wasn't that simple. It wasn't about strange roads and poetry. It was about drugs.

"And Rafe?"

"He's not using drugs. Not now, anyway. But he's running the streets and I'm afraid for him. I keep telling him all the things I should have been telling myself," she said.

No. I wasn't buying it. "Gabi. Gabi. When I say your name, it's more than a name. It's what I think about love. It's what I feel about family. Maybe you've been my idea of a road or a path. And now I'm so confused. It's like . . . it's like you hurt someplace but you don't even know where you hurt."

"Oh, Spoon, I don't want to hurt you. . . ." She was crying. Deep animal noises came out of her and she was clutching at my arms and my chest, as if she wanted me desperately but was afraid to hold on. "Let me . . . let me put the words on paper. I'll burn them into the paper for you. I need to get all the words right. Give me that chance, Spoon. I'll see you tomorrow, or the next day. You'll make me say the words and it'll make me get it back in order. Please. Please."

I took Gabi to her door. "Do you want me to come up?"

"No, I need you to be away from me, and think about me," she said. "Right now you're asking me why I'm messing up my life and I don't have anything to say that's neat and clean and logical. I see you looking at me and I want to tear my heart out when I see the disappointment in your face. God knows I want to be special for you, Spoon. God can see my heart and He knows I want to be special for you."

"You are special, Gabi. You are special."

Good night. Lips touching lightly, Gabi's head against my chest, moving away from me ever so slowly, as if she were afraid to let go.

I took the train uptown. By the time I reached 145th it was raining. A woman asked if I had two quarters to spare. I was offended. I walked away and instantly felt guilty, too guilty to turn around and give her the two quarters, which is what I wanted to do.

Mom was doing a crossword puzzle. She asked me how Gabi was doing.

"Not well," I said. "Can you know where a person is, and still think they're lost?"

"I know you care for her," she said, "but . . ." Kindly, she let the words trail off. But they were there in the night air and we both knew we would find them again.

THE STOOP — 145TH STREET

The light on Christmas morning was a harsh gray. From beyond my bedroom window, there were dueling radios. I recognized Handel. When I got up to go to the bathroom, my parents were already in the kitchen, and I was greeted by the comforting smell of freshly brewed coffee. The cold water on my face felt good. I told myself I would have a wonderful day.

"Are you up?" Mom called.

"Will be in a minute!" I called back.

Sitting on the edge of the bed, I told myself not to go to Gabi's. I knew how it would go: Rafe answering the door, telling me he'd get Gabi, then coming back and saying she'd call me later from the pay phone on the corner.

She wouldn't call.

I thought of the sweater I'd bought her from the school store. It had a big W on the front for Wallingford, but I had planned to tell her that it stood for Witherspoon. We were supposed to laugh.

I looked at myself in the mirror above my bureau, and saw that my eyes were teary. Did crying come so easy? When had it started sneaking up on me so naturally?

I had coffee with my parents. Mom made nice-nice over the book I'd bought her, and Dad, somehow, was touched by the football I gave him. They gave me a great fountain pen. We chatted quietly through the morning, like three friends, and it felt good. Later, no longer able to bear the silent telephone, I went back to bed.

"Yeah, Christmas was okay," I said. Scott and I were sitting on the stoop, edging our way into a conversation, when Lavelle came over and asked us to unload some groceries from a truck. Lavelle, tall, black, his head shiny bald. He had been looking out for kids on the block for as long as I could remember. Like all old men on the block, he expected us to know something.

"I got to get the truck back downtown," he said. "It won't take you no time and you got ten dollars apiece."

I liked doing stuff with Scott so I said okay and we went to the back of the rental truck. Lavelle had a helper from his little restaurant come out with a handcart to help us.

"So, man, we need some serious hangout time," Scott said. He was on the truck handing out boxes of frozen fish. They were wet and stinky.

"Your mom tell you that I called?"

"Yeah, she did." Scott tried to pick up two boxes at once, then put one down. There were a lot more boxes than we'd thought there would be. "We went to services yesterday and she asked me if I had called you."

"Yo, where do you think Lavelle got all these frozen fish?"

"I don't know," Scott said. "I don't think his refrigerator is big enough for all of them, either."

The helper was standing on the sidewalk next to the handcart and I asked him if he was crippled. He caught an attitude and said something under his breath, but he didn't help with the unloading, just the wheeling of the boxes into the restaurant.

"You see Gabriela?" Scott called down.

"Yeah, have you seen her around much?" My stomach tightened.

73

"No, I don't get downtown and you know I left school."

Left school? I didn't answer. No, I didn't know he had left school. Scott was my main man. We had been tight for years. When I left we had promised to write to each other, but we hadn't. Somehow I was always too busy, or too tired, or didn't have anything to say. The weeks had slipped by, and then the months, and then we were on the block unloading frozen fish.

"When did you leave school, man?"

"Right after midterms," he said. "A bunch of us left then."

"Why?"

All at once the street was filled with noise. A blast from a siren. Brakes screeching. Startled, I looked around. Two dark cars had stopped, one with its front tires on the sidewalk. Men were jumping out of the cars, guns in the air.

"On the ground! On the ground!"

I fell to the ground and put my hands out by my sides. I could feel my heart racing.

"Don't move! Don't move!"

"Yo, Spoon, it's not us." I heard Scott's voice next to me and sensed his body. I realized I had shut my eyes. I opened them, looked up, and saw a crowd on the sidewalk.

I got up and saw that the men with the guns had badges

on chains around their necks. Some of the guns were still drawn. In between the sea of legs, there were two people on the ground.

"That's Leon," Scott said.

Leon. Good jump shot. Couldn't handle fractions.

"Man, get my fish unloaded before it goes bad," Lavelle hissed.

I was wondering if the fish was stolen. Why was it in a rental truck? Scott got back up in the truck and we continued to unload it as the commotion on the sidewalk played out. I saw they had Leon against the wall. One cop had his knee in Leon's back and was pushing him against the wall while the others searched him. There was a struggle on the ground with the other person.

The truck was half unloaded. The rest of the food was canned groceries. I was relieved. Why was I relieved to see cans instead of frozen fish?

The next thing I knew Leon was handcuffed with his hands behind his back. A cop, young, white, tough-looking, held the cuffs high, forcing Leon to bend over. They rushed him into the back of one of the cars. The guy on the ground was lifted to his feet. It was Ray. There was dog crap on the front of his shirt.

Ray. Couldn't play no b-ball but could sing up a storm. Had all the finest ladies.

They spun him around, bent him over, and finished searching him. Ray fell and the cops, finding nothing on him, took off the handcuffs and left him lying on the sidewalk. They got into their cars and in a moment squealed away toward Frederick Douglass Boulevard.

"Welcome home, brother," Scott said.

"Is Leon dealing?" I asked.

"Guess what? I don't keep tabs on all the dealers," Scott said. He seemed offended. He wouldn't have been offended before I left.

We finished unloading the boxes in silence and Lavelle asked us how much he had promised us. Neither one of us answered him and he "remembered" that it was ten apiece.

Back on the stoop, Scott was kidding about me getting on the ground.

"You're out of the 'hood two days and you forget the routine," he joked.

I was grinning but uncomfortable. Down the street, in front of the record store, Ray was talking to a small crowd. He had taken off his shirt and thrown it into the gutter. Some men from the barbershop had come out and stood at the edge of the group.

I turned back to Scott. "Hey, man, you never did tell me why you left school."

"I decided to go to Cooper Union at nights," he said. "Get right into the arts thing. I needed some money to get started next September."

"How are you going to Cooper Union if you don't finish Douglass?"

"Just taking some art courses so I can get a j-o-b," he said. There was a studied casualness to his gestures as he spoke. "Maybe I'll go to regular college later. But what I want to do is art. Most artists don't finish college. You know, my thing isn't that conventional. I mean, my vision has changed. I'm seeing behind objects and through them. I'm still into the drafting thing, I know I can draw, but what I want to see is what makes something beautiful, or what makes it ugly. I can't learn that in school; I have to get it out here in the streets."

I didn't understand him and left it there. The silence that crept between us was heavy, cumbersome, and we both changed positions to deal with it. Scott drew up his legs; I leaned back and put my hands behind my neck. More silence as we searched for words that we might want to say.

"So what's up with Wallingford?" he finally asked.

"Just about what we thought. Rich white kids, some

Asians, a few of us. They run it like a college more than a high school. It's okay."

"You miss Douglass?"

"Yeah, a little." I wondered if he would have left if I had stayed at Douglass. I didn't want to ask.

"Things are the same on the block," he said. "I bet if we went back in time fifty years, and came to this block, it would be the same. Just different people. Maybe fewer cars. Other than that it's just everybody drifting into the same ol' same ol'. Running down their raps about why they're watching the world go by."

We watched as some of the guys who were talking on the sidewalk started to drift into the barbershop. Scott tapped my elbow and pointed to where Ray had thrown his shirt. A dog was peeing on it and we both laughed.

"Suppose that fish was stolen," Scott said. "And we were arrested. Can you imagine how that would look on the front page of *The New York Times*? 'Frozen Trout Thieves Busted in Harlem!' You could never live that down."

"So how are you going to get a job in art?"

"What are you, the FBI now?"

I didn't answer. A beat. Scott put his hand on my knee and rocked it gently. "I don't know, man." His voice sounded like a huge sigh. "My life is getting raggedy. Nothing much seemed to happen. It just slid from correct to raggedy."

"Everything is looking so different to me," I said. "Hear Clara is pregnant?"

"Yeah." He shook his head. "She was like a symbol of all the right things to do."

"So, let me try this on you —" Ball in the left hand, stop, pivot, fake right, ball in the right hand. "Why don't you come up to Wallingford one weekend and take a look around. I can find you a place to squat."

"Sure, that sounds good." Scott stretched his legs. "I can get to meet all the preppies."

I would have liked to have Scott come to the Academy, to see the pond, the grounds, maybe to sit and rap with me in Hill House. I would have loved even more for things to have been as easy as they used to be with us, so I could tell him about Gabi. *Gabi is using.* I wanted to say the words to somebody, to hear them coming from my lips so I could try to make sense of it.

"It's not all that," I said. "I mean, Wallingford, it's not all that."

"You like it?"

"Yeah. I like it. I haven't checked out all the corners yet. I'm still one eyeing into the fish store, but I think I like it."

Two kids, maybe three or four years old, playing with a pink rubber ball, knocked it toward us. Scott grabbed it and just crossed his arms. One of the kids, big eyed, looked at me and then at Scott and took a tentative step toward us "big guys." Scott stared the kid down until he put both hands behind his back.

"You want this ball?" Scott asked. He tried to look mean, but he was smiling.

The kid nodded and Scott held it out. The kid approached slowly, grabbed the ball, and then gave Scott a defiant look.

"A baby gangster," I said.

Scott pointed down the street. I looked and saw Leon going into the barbershop.

"Let's check out what's happening," Scott said.

Inside Leon was already telling his story.

"So they said a guy who looks like me ripped off some valuable baseball cards from a white dude downtown." The left side of Leon's face was swollen and his words weren't clear. "So they're saying they heard I sold baseball cards at the flea market and what did I know about this dude's cards. I didn't know nothing about the cards."

"You were never officially arrested?" A heavy dude in horn-rimmed glasses.

"No," Leon said. "They just said I better let them know if I see the cards."

"So, we'll file a report," Horn-rimmed said.

"What good is that going to do?" Leon asked.

"It's going to say that the New York Police Department cannot just slam people around and terrorize people without a response," Horn-rimmed replied. "And that might not do any good. And it begins a proceeding that will lead to a police department hearing and that might not do any good. But it will also show a community unity, a willingness to stake our claim for this neighborhood, and that will do some good."

The young brothers talked about what they really wanted to do, but they were deferential to the men in the barbershop.

Scott and I went back to the stoop. All along the street there were small groups of young men standing and talking. And watching. They were a little stronger now that the elders were involved.

"You hear anybody say who Clara is going with?" I asked.

"The tide," Scott said. "Things drift with the tide and she drifted with it."

The tide. I was hearing talk of tides that drift and carry

people away, of roads that turn into mazes, of paths that disappeared.

"So much has been going on in the 'hood since I was gone it makes me feel funny," I said.

"You see something going on?" Scott asked, looking away from me. There was a sadness in his voice that couldn't be answered.

RIVERSIDE DRIVE AND 96TH STREET

Riverside Park was bright and cheerful. Big-eyed, round-faced kids ran in wild circles, showing off their new Christmas toys. I tried to put everything in its place, to make everything seem right. Gabi was wearing the sweater I had given her under her parka. She was beautiful again. With the cascades of children's laughter as a backdrop, I imagined what our child might look like. Perhaps a girl lighter than me, darker than Gabi, and beautiful. Earlier there had been a few snow flurries, which I'd hoped would decorate the park for us, but they had given way to a light, chilling rain.

"You seem different today," I said.

"How?" Gabi asked.

"You've brought our lunch in a bag, you're smiling, you seem so happy."

"'*Cuando yo te estoy cantando, en la Tierra acaba el mal. . . .*'" Gabi leaned her head against my shoulder. "'When I am singing to you, all the evil in the world stops.'"

I wanted to believe her. I held her hand and squeezed it, wanting the moment to last forever, wanting evil to end. There were a lot of children in the park. They were all brown. Even the white ones seemed somehow on the verge of brown.

"I think I'd like to have three children."

Gabi put her hand over her mouth. "I am so surprised at you, Spoon! Only women are supposed to think things like that."

"I don't even know why I said it."

"Children are innocence," Gabi said, sounding suddenly very serious. "Sometimes I see myself with a child and being very happy. Then sometimes I see myself looking at a child and wondering what right I have to such an innocent person. I believe that if you have a child, you must either put that child in a frame, put a label on it immediately, or wait to discover who she is. If you wait, then you have to be afraid. The child will be a stranger, looking at you with no evil in their heart. Looking at you as if they wanted you to share their innocence."

Where are you going, Gabi? What do you want to tell me?

Skateboarders. Five in a row, their first doing his tricks, the others following, trying to copy the leader. He was good. Gabi stopped and watched them. Her face was serious, almost stern. Then she turned away with a wave of the hand. Skateboarding was not the stuff of life.

The drizzle had let up. We stopped and sat on a bench. Gabi took a tinfoil dish and a thermos jug out of a plastic shopping bag. There were fried chicken wings and potato salad and yellow Filipino bread. We ate and she told me what our child would be like.

"If he is like you he will be too serious. Even when he's in diapers he's going to be too serious," she said. "And he's going to wear glasses."

"I don't wear glasses."

"He's going to wear glasses just to prove he's more serious than you."

"What are we going to do?" I asked.

"Two things." Gabi held up two fingers. "First, we have

his glasses tinted, which will at least make him look cooler. Then we get him a baby girlfriend, maybe one of those little cuties in the soap commercials. She'll loosen him up."

"I meant about us," I said.

"Whatever you want."

"I can't do whatever I want if I don't know what's going on with you, Gabi. We can't just say that everything is the same. It's not."

Tears. *Lagrimas*. She had given me the word years ago. I had said something wrong to her, had hurt her, and she had written it down on a piece of paper and handed it to me. "*Lagrimas*," she had said, pointing to the tears that streamed down her face. "Hold on to them."

Now her tears screamed at me. *What do you want?* they shouted. *Why are you looking at me like that? Where are your answers?* I put my arm around her and she leaned against me.

"How's your mother?" I asked, searching for neutral ground.

"Worse," Gabi answered. "The doctor thinks she doesn't have the will to live. She's hallucinating. Yesterday I went to see her and she said that my father had just been there. I know he has never gone to see her.

"They say that she can come home soon. I know it's because they can't do anything more for her. It's sad, but whatever happens will happen and I'm ready for it. Maybe you'll come with me to the hospital. You have the stomach for it?"

"Sure." I didn't want to go.

"I got the phone put back in. It's mostly for my mother. I don't want her to die without speaking . . ." She paused, then pulled herself together. "I don't want her to die without speaking."

"To say good-bye?"

"Or whatever troubles her mind," Gabi said.

I didn't know Lucila, Gabi's mother. She was a shadow woman, always standing just out of the light, never quite in focus when I looked for her. I was sorry that she was dying. I was sorry that she would die without me ever really knowing her. I tried to push her death out of my mind as I walked Gabi home.

When I kissed her at the door Gabi said she had been sure that I was going to hit on her when I came home.

"Do you think about me that way?" she asked, standing against her door in the dim hallway. "Do you want to do nasty things to me?"

"Yes," I said, sliding my hand down from her shoulder.

She took my hand, the one seeking its own adventure, and kissed it.

WEST END AVENUE, ST. MARK'S SCHOOL GYMNASIUM

The narrow running track ran in a tight circle under stained glass windows that badly needed washing. Below the track the gymnasium floor, some of the boards along the wall lifting from the hard bed beneath, was unpolished and uneven where indifferent repairs had been made over the years. There were dead spots where the ball wouldn't bounce properly and the curvature of the track prevented shots from the corners. I thought about the athletic center at Wallingford with its synthetic surface and natural lighting.

Brand had tried twice to set up the game before getting it on. He was a whiner and I also thought he was a snob but somehow I had found myself in the same circles he was in at the Academy. He had picked up three other white guys, one who looked to be six five or so, and me. The "team" we were going to be playing against was all black. One of them was the son of the janitor at Brand's apartment and that's how the game got started. We were playing at St. Mark's because the guy was also the janitor there and had the use of the gym at night. I didn't mind playing ball, not even with Brand, but for some reason it annoyed me to see Chanelle and Amy show up with him.

Brand had himself playing point guard with me at one of the forward positions. On defense he wanted to run a two-one-two zone, which was all right with me, because it forced a pattern to the game that could be useful.

Brand introduced me to the janitor's son, in his mid-twenties, with a round moon of a face that flowed effortlessly into his double chins. He said his name was Wilson without differentiating whether it was a first or last name.

"Where you live?"

"A hundred forty-fifth," I said.

He said he used to have an aunt who lived near 145th and I said, "Oh, good."

Brand gave us a silly pep talk, unofficially designating himself as captain, and the game was on.

Wilson's team consisted of two kids who looked like they could have been fourteen or younger, and two men who were at least thirty. One of them wore long shorts down to his knees. They brought the ball down first and they looked like a mixed bag. The dude with the ball dribbled it through his legs for no reason, made useless passes as if he were trying to set something up, tried a drive between two defenders, then threw up a twisting jump shot that missed the rim altogether.

The guys who Brand brought had played together. One of them had mentioned Trinity, the Episcopal prep school, and I figured that all of them might have played there. They were good, not great, but they didn't throw the ball away.

Wilson couldn't play, but he hustled, a jerky, awkward kind of hustle that was all knees and elbows and sweat popping off. I found myself on him several times, pushing him away from the basket with my chest, and him not having enough floor moves to get around me.

Chanelle and Amy were keeping time. It was supposed to be two twenty-two-minute periods with no time-outs.

Amy marked off the period by running onto the court, waving her arms, and pointing at her watch. Even with us having the biggest man on the court and fewer turnovers we were only up by three points, 31–28, at the end of the first period.

We sat down and Brand started in his whine about how far ahead we would have been if we were calling fouls.

"I think I would have had at least nine foul shots," he said.

I was wishing Scott were there. He would have been the best player on the court.

The second half started with us in a one-two-two. They had only taken a couple of outside shots the first half and so I thought it would probably work. As it turned out Wilson and another of their players pooped out after five minutes and were bent over, with their hands on their knees, gasping for air. I thought that the whole game would cool out. I was wrong. Brand and the other three guys on my team were suddenly more intense, calling plays instead of freelancing, setting harder picks, pushing the score way past the point that they were going to be caught. I wanted to laugh when one of them started calling numbered defenses, as if we were playing some professional team in the playoffs. They weren't just winning a game, they were beating a team they would talk about during the school year, elevating the level of competition in their conversation as if they had really taken on and conquered some real players. I imagined phrases: "These street hustlers from the city," or "Some mean black dudes that tried to beat us to death." Basketball as a landscape for white triumph.

Game over. Final score 58–38. High fives all around. The guarded landscape of advantage and winning. Chanelle and Amy congratulated us. Wilson's team came over to where we were putting on our street shirts and shook our hands.

"You guys were kicking some butt at the end," Wilson said.

I looked to see if he was serious. He was and I moved away from him, uncomfortable with his accommodating the situation.

Brand was going home with one of the Trinity players. He said he'd call me if we played again. We shook hands, with me deciding that after thinking they were making too much of the game, I was doing the same thing. Wilson was checking the windows as we began to drift out to Amsterdam Avenue.

"They're probably going to drink beer," Chanelle said. "Come on by my place and get some ice cream. You feel like walking?"

I had arranged to go to Gabi's house at six and then to the hospital to see her mother. It was three, and I wanted to shower and told Chanelle so. She suggested that I shower at her house.

"My mother's not going to mind," she said.

Somewhere in the back of my mind a dormant layer of lust was stirred. I tried to disassociate it from Chanelle, telling myself that I had time to kill and, perhaps truthfully, that I didn't want to tell my mother that I was going to the hospital with Gabi. Mom already suspected that all wasn't right between Gabi and me. She didn't know what was wrong, but her ears were perked and waiting for any opening.

We took the number 1 train down to 59th Street and walked the five blocks to Chanelle's house. I was thinkng about a hundred things as we entered the building. I wasn't thinking about the doorman. His eyes pierced me, and I looked away.

"I'm really looking forward to going back to school," she said in the elevator. "I just want to get this new semester going and do some serious thinking before I start college."

"You decide on a major yet?"

"My dad is pushing finance, and I think that's just because my mom is so lame with money. He's working the same strings. Get back at her through me. My brother wants me to get into home decorating — you know he's studying architecture at UCLA?"

"Yes." Into her apartment.

"He's got some idea that we could go into business together. But that home decoration is so, like, the little woman's thing. I don't want any part of it. You want me to get you a clean T-shirt from my brother's room?"

"Sure, how big is he?"

"He's big," she said.

In the bathroom I took off my shirt and T-shirt. Something told me to leave. Chanelle was talking on a cell phone as she handed the shirt to me.

"You want to go out for dinner?" she said into the phone. "About nine or so? Okay, see you then."

I held up the T-shirt and it looked to be my size.

I felt Chanelle's arms around my waist and saw her head as she looked around me into the bathroom mirror. She was smiling, making a funny face, giving me a chance to back away. I grasped her two hands in one of mine and held them together, lifted one arm, and turned around so that I was facing her. The smile was less silly as she looked into my eyes.

"Can I reach your lips if we're both standing?" I asked.

She lifted her arms and pulled my head down to hers. Then we were kissing, and then she was pushing me away.

"We'd better cool down," she said. "Why don't you take a shower and I'll have the ice cream ready when you're finished."

"You sure you don't want to take a shower with me?"

"No, I'm not sure," she said. "But I won't go all the way, so I'd better not start taking anything off."

She backed out of the bathroom and closed the door.

I was dizzy with wanting her. A dozen scenarios flickered through my mind. Chanelle coming back into the bathroom, into the shower. Me coming out with just a towel wrapped around my waist. The two of us going into her room.

The warm water didn't help and I turned the cold water up until my shoulders were covered with goose pimples. More scenarios danced through my mind, this time with the scenes of lust interlaced with scenes of her father coming through the door in a rage. Why did I imagine him with such a large head?

I showered for as long as I could stand it, saw that Chanelle was not going to make an instant move, dressed, and came out to find her watching television.

"The ice cream was brick hard," she said. "It's edible now."

"Should I be sorry I kissed you?" I asked.

"I'm not," she said. "But I'm sure you knew that."

Where was my head? As I ate the ice cream I couldn't think of anything but wanting Chanelle. It didn't make any difference what we were doing, as long as she was female and I was male and we were alone.

"Why are you smiling?" she asked.

"I'm surprised at how you make me feel," I said.

"We're going to have to be very careful when we get back to school," she said, smiling. "I don't want to get pregnant in my senior year."

Careful? Pregnant? What was she suggesting? That we would be a couple at Wallingford? That we would be lovers?

We sat on the edge of the couch, with Chanelle sitting in the corner and turned to me, and me sitting on the middle cushions. Our knees touched lightly, now and again, as we spoke quietly. I traced small circles in the palm of her hand with my middle finger. I wanted to say something with the weight of the moment, but my thoughts flickered nervously, like the dying neon sign that spelled out Pentecostal on a storefront church I could see from my kitchen window when I was a kid. Where Chanelle's hard body pushed against the fabric of her jeans, Gabi's thin body retreated beneath the unseasonably light clothing she wore. I thought of Gabi as I stumbled uneasily between my thoughts of her and my body's memory of pressing against Chanelle.

"Sometimes the senior year can really be stressful," she said. "You end up getting into situations you don't want to be in."

"You smell nice," I said. "A hint of flowers."

"You smell like soap," she said. And then, "Do you think you might want to join the choir? I love your voice."

"Could be," I said. "We'll see."

For a moment we were silent, and close to each other. I saw her eyes, brown, baby-doll wide, a strong lower lip making her look older than the roundness of her face suggested.

Time for me to leave, and she walked me to the door. We worked at being casual as we walked to the elevator. As the doors opened she kissed me again and murmured that we would have to be careful when we got back to the Academy.

On the way out I stopped for a moment to return the doorman's look. It was unexpected and he raised his eyes to the ceiling.

I was in a different world, and it was easy to be in. The paths were somehow clearer downtown. At 59th Street, still lust high, I took the uptown train.

LA PLUMITA, DOMINICAN REPUBLIC

Rafe let me in and then told me he had to leave. The old man was sitting at the kitchen table, a half a cup of tea in front of him. The teabag, carefully laid on the paper it had come in, was next to the cup.

"Gabi in?"

"She'll be back soon," Rafe said, glancing at the old man, "any minute. I have to run to the store."

I watched as Rafe nervously scooped change from the top of the refrigerator. He was a blur as he rushed past me and, over his footsteps already in the hall, I heard him calling that he would be back shortly.

"I'm Anthony Witherspoon, sir," I said. I reached out

my hand for his, realized he didn't see it, and brought it back to my side. "We've met before."

No response.

"I'm Gabi's . . . friend," I said.

He nodded.

"Do you mind if I sit?"

He gestured, a palm turned that said "If you please," and I sat across from him. Immediately I searched for conversation. He was blind and couldn't comfort himself with visual judgments. He had to listen, and I didn't have any words.

The red second hand of the clock on the wall moved silently. Five seconds. Ten. Fifteen. An eternity.

"It's not that cold today," I said. "Yesterday was a lot colder."

He nodded slowly. His face was not brown, but suggested brown. He was lighter than Gabi, and I imagined him walking arm in arm with a tall black woman. He was handsome and she sensuous. Immediately my mind switched to Chanelle.

"Who are your parents?" he asked.

My parents. "My father's name is Sidney and he works for the Internal Revenue Service in Brooklyn. My mother, Eloyce, works for a finance company."

"And they are who they work for!" He hit his fist lightly on the table. "That means they are Americans!"

We both laughed.

"When I was young I wanted so to come to New York. I was teaching English and geography in La Plumita — that's how things are done there — and I had seen drawings by a Cuban artist, Miguel Covarrubias. I said to myself, could these people be so free, so alive with all that I had heard about them? I wanted to know. But in my city, La Plumita, there was no way for me to find out.

"I thought — it was a young man's thought — that if I ever got to San Pedro I would find out. San Pedro was only eight miles away, but it took my family twenty years after they first thought about it to move from La Plumita to San Pedro. Then they hated it."

"Why?"

"Because it was different from La Plumita," he said. "For a simple people *la diferencia* is enough. But I still wondered about America. What I knew about your country was New York, Hollywood — and I thought it was two words — and where the black people lived."

"Harlem," I said.

"Now I am come here and I can't see it," he said. "I

don't know if there are mountains here, or lakes. I don't know if swallows go from tree to tree all day."

"There aren't any mountains or lakes in Harlem," I said. "Take my word for it."

"But those are your words," he said. "Those are the visions you have seen. It means nothing to me. My only visions are of La Plumita and of San Pedro."

"They're good visions, I hope."

"They are wonderful. I am a romantic. And so I see my grandmother, she was so small, working in our garden. We called her Chiquitina and she loved it. Each morning she would go to the well and draw fresh water and then she would come home and work in the garden. The garden was special to us. My father, a rather hard man, would work all day in a factory that made rum to send to the United States. When he came home he loved to sit in the garden and hold his guitar across his lap."

"He enjoyed playing the guitar?" The old man was fishing, but for what?

"He couldn't play, but he enjoyed holding it in case God would send down a miracle."

"You never saw him play?"

"What did I see? Now that I am blind I ask myself that

question a hundred times a day. What did I see? Did I really see fields ten acres wide swaying with lilies? Were all the women in La Plumita really so beautiful? Or am I seeing now with my heart what I never saw with my eyes? When the boy leaves in a rush all that I see is a shadow across my eyes. From then on it is what the heart sees."

"Teenagers are always rushing someplace," I said. He was telling me that his heart saw something wrong. Did he think I'd tell him what it was?

"When we're young we think we have to hurry," he said. "When we're old and to the place to which we were rushing, we know we didn't have to bother."

"Sometimes I wonder what I'm seeing," I said. "The place I go to school, in Connecticut, is so different from Harlem. I come back here and I'm seeing things that I've never seen before."

"There is a danger whenever you go back to a place that you remember from a distance," he said. "The danger is that you only look with your eyes. You see a friend you haven't seen in twenty years and what happens? You see an old man and not the swimming together on early mornings. You see a woman with a limp and forget how you shared a piece of fruit with that same woman when you were young.

"The eyes are not always faithful to the heart. Are you seeing with your heart?"

"I'm not sure what I'm seeing with."

"Not being sure is good, too," he said. "Do you want me to make tea?"

"No, do you want me to make tea?"

"No, do you want me to make tea?"

We laughed again. I liked him and, I thought, he liked me. I watched him as he got up, found the teapot, and filled it with water.

"In the center of La Plumita there is a town square," he said. "On Sunday nights everyone came there. Young girls dressed in their finest, young men in clean shirts and slicked-back hair, families. The old women would sit and watch the young girls, to make sure they acted decently. If you lived in that little town you could tell your age by what you did in the square on Sunday evenings. If you played with your friends, you were a boy. If you put oil in your hair and washed your hands ten times to get the dirt from under your fingernails, you were a man. Then, if you just sat and rested, wondering how Sunday, your day off, had gone by so quickly, you were a family man."

"It sounds like a good life," I said.

"But was it true?" He tilted his head back and I saw that his eyes were grayed over. "Was any of it true, or is my heart as blind as my eyes?"

"I think it's true."

We waited and the small talk between us became smaller and smaller. The tea grew cold. An hour went by and then another. Twice he asked me the time, and I told him. I wondered where Gabi was. Was she rushing through the darkness, her smooth walk a jazz adagio over the asphalt streets? Did the moonless December night frighten her? Our minds, mine and the old man's, were rushing about the small kitchen. Finally, I said to him that I should be going home.

"Your parents will be worried about you," he said, nodding.

"My mother worries about me even when I'm in the house," I said.

"Ah, that's who she is," he said, "not a job."

I took the subway uptown. The car I was in was nearly empty and I started to read a newspaper I found on one of the seats but thoughts of Gabi distracted me. She seemed so different than she had been, as if she had been somehow wound tighter than a person ever should be, as if any moment she would either spring loose into a thousand

parts or stop altogether. Somehow I had lost my understanding of her.

I found my parents watching television. My dad asked
me how things were going, and I said they were going well.

"I guess you're ready to get back to school?" he said, not
looking at me.

"Not that ready," I said, glancing at Mom.

I was tired and thought about going right to bed, but I
knew what my father was saying, that I hadn't spent much
time with them. I stayed up and we talked about the television shows we were watching. Mom laughed too hard at all
my comments and Dad was being distant, cool. I only had
a few days left before I had to go back to school. I made
myself some promises to hang out with my folks.

Dad went to bed first, and I sat next to Mom on the
couch and put my arm around her.

"Watch it," she said. "I'm a married woman."

I was dreaming when my father woke me. The lights were
on in my bedroom and for a moment I didn't know where I
was. My father's shaking was strenuous, urgent.

"What's up?"

"Grab the phone," he said. "It's that girl."

The phone was on the dresser, and I swung my feet over

the side of the bed to reach it. In the mirror I saw my father watching me closely.

"Hello?"

"Spoon. Spoon. I'm sorry to call you so late, honey." Gabi's speech was slow, distant. "What time is it?"

"I don't know what time it is," I said.

"Four-fifteen," my father said.

"It's four-fifteen," I repeated. "Where are you?"

"I'm at a girlfriend's house," she said. "Mami died last night."

The image of a thin woman, her dark hair pinned away from a face that seemed too young to belong to my girl-friend's mother, flickered through my mind.

"Gabi, why don't you go home?" I said. "Are you all right? Can you go home?"

"I'm on my way home now," she said. "Will you come by later?"

"Yes, of course. You were with her?"

"I was sitting by the bed. I think I dozed off and . . . oh, man. Spoon, I'm broken. I'm broken!"

"Gabi, you have to . . ." No, there was nothing that she *had* to do. "Do you want me to come over — I'll come over now."

"No. Wait until I call you. Give me some time. Let me tell Abuelo," she said. "I'll see you later, baby."

The phone went dead and I hung up.

"She drunk?" my father asked.

"Her mother died last night," I said.

"And she was drinking?"

"It sounded like it," I said, almost sure that she was high, but not from booze.

"You need to wait until daylight before you go over there," my father said. He loosened the belt on his robe and refastened it. "Nothing you can do right now."

"I think you're right," I said.

My father took my hand. "You need me, I'm there for you, Anthony," he said. "You want me to shut out the light?"

I nodded and he flicked the switch. In the darkness I thought about Gabi. She had called me "baby." It was too small a word for her. I had seen people high before, fading in and out, hanging on to the surface chatter to communicate.

Gabi, I am so sorry your mother died, and I am so afraid for you. I am so afraid for you.

The sun was coming through my window when I woke again. My parents were already at the table. My father

107

asked if I wanted him to stay home. He said he had some sick days coming. I said no, but that I appreciated him offering. Mom had to leave for work first and Dad asked me again if I wanted him to stay. Again I said no.

I showered and rummaged through my closet until I found a decent pair of pants to wear. The street was just coming to life when I got downstairs. The super was wrestling some garbage to the curb; across the street a delivery truck was already unloading cases of soda at the grocery store. The rest of the world was going about its business.

Gabi would need comforting, I knew. So would the old man. I remembered that Gabi had an aunt who sold advertising for *La Prensa,* a Spanish-language newspaper. But what did she know about Gabi?

THE LABYRINTH

A cold December morning. People leaned into the wind as they maneuvered the hill toward the 145th Street station. In the station there were still touches of holiday spirit. Somebody had put up a mural of children's drawings, which brought smiles. The new year was only days away and there were still touches of Christmas color among the otherwise dark clothing of the huddled passengers. A few of the women were carrying shopping bags, and I imagined they contained goodies for office parties.

The downtown train was a mixture of rumble and

squeal as it jerked its way into the station. People positioned themselves to get on, shifting their weight, pushing toward the doors while being careful not to violate the tiny cocoon of personal space each demanded. I allowed myself to be herded onto the train and grabbed the overhead rail. As the doors closed I felt a slight chill, and then an uneasiness in the pit of my stomach that made me think I would throw up. For a second I thought it was the lack of air in the jammed car, but then I realized that it was not just nausea that I felt, it was fear.

Gabi and I had always been there for each other, had always managed to understand each other's feelings, and find the right words to reassure and help. But we hadn't dealt with drugs before, or death. We had always projected our lives onto a larger, more expansive screen, one which we could paint with the comfortable background of what would happen next and the immediacy of the poetry we shared. Now we were coping with the here and now. Where once we were living largely in the realm of our collective imaginations, now we were forced to live in the present, and the present had no promise of forgiveness.

I got off at 125th and walked toward Gabi's apartment. From somewhere I conjured up a scene in which I was holding Gabi, and she was crying and explaining how her mother's death had torn something from her. We would hold each other, be impossibly close to each other, and things would be all right again.

When I crossed Manhattan Avenue I saw Rafe walking down the block away from me and I called his name. He turned, saw me, and waited.

"I got milk for coffee," he announced, holding up the container in a plastic bag. "You seen Gabi?"

"She's not home?"

"She hasn't been home since the day before yesterday," he said. "I don't know where she is."

"Hey, Rafe. I'm sorry about your mom, man. You okay?"

"Yeah, I guess."

"Look, you hang in there. I'll look for Gabi," I said. "Any idea where she might be? She called me early this morning and said she was at a girlfriend's house."

"I don't hang with her," he said, shrugging.

"Yo, Rafe, you know Gabi's using, right?" I was attempting to put on my Harlem street voice but it came out hesitantly, weak.

Rafe looked down the street and I was almost tempted to look in the same direction, too, to see what he might be searching for.

"Yeah, man, I know, but I don't know where she gets her stuff or nothing," Rafe said.

We stood for a brief and awkward eternity, shifting our weights on the corner, as the condensation from our breaths mingled and dissipated in the morning air. I sensed that Rafe was not all that concerned with Gabi, or even with his mother's death. He had his own demons to contend with.

"Tell your grandfather I'll call when I find her," I said. "You going to be around the house today?"

He gave me an unconvincing "Yeah" and headed up the street.

Where to start looking? Gabi had called at a little after four, saying she was at a friend's house, and I didn't think anything had happened to her. I tried to imagine her high, and pushed my thoughts away from it. It was too soon to call the police or even the hospital. Nothing came to mind except to walk around places that I knew she liked. I went over to Mt. Morris Park and remembered the days we'd spent there. Once she had asked me to come with her to the park and to bring some poetry. We'd sat on one of the benches and read to each other. I had read Derek Walcott and she had read some short pieces by a Cuban poet, Carolina Hospital. We were enjoying the poems and each other, and then she had announced that she had one more poem for me, one that she had written, and then we would have to leave.

"Don't ask me to translate the poem into English," Gabi had said, taking my face in her hands. "I'd be too embarrassed."

The words she'd recited, ever so slowly, just above a whisper, in a language that I couldn't reach, had so filled me that day, I'd become suddenly heroic, had been able to fly, to soar over the familiar gray of the city into the heavens. It was when I had loved her the most.

I sat on the same bench and watched as pigeons pecked at a dirty bag near the water fountain.

I didn't think she would be at St. Cecilia's, but I went over there anyway. I told myself that I was doing the right thing, no matter how fruitless it seemed. What I wanted was for her to just show up, alive and well, and ready to restart the business of living, no matter how painful. I hoped that she would lean on me, and that I would be strong enough to carry the weight of her grieving.

One Hundred and Twenty-fifth Street. How many times had we walked down this street solving the problems of the world? It was already crowded. I went east until I reached Park Avenue. There were sidewalk evangelists already preaching on the corners, some day workers with their toolboxes waiting to be picked up, a man with a grocery store shopping cart filled with scrap metal rummaging through some discarded boxes.

On one corner there was a woman, incredibly thin, her dark skin dull and pockmarked, nodding out on the corner. She leaned to one side, her eyes closed, and dipped to an impossible angle before jerking herself upright. People walked by her as if she wasn't there. A patrol car cruised past and the policeman turned his head away from her. I watched as I glanced at a clock in a bodega window and saw that it was ten-thirty.

I walked and walked. I called Gabi's house at one, and then again at four. She hadn't shown up.

Gabi's mom had died late Wednesday, she had called me Thursday morning, and no one had seen her since, or heard from her. I called the house and spoke to her grandfather twice and I could hear the hurt in his voice. He told me the funeral was to be Tuesday afternoon at St. Joseph's and asked me if I knew where it was. Yes, of course, I had passed it on 125th and St. Nicholas a thousand times. Yes, I would be there for the funeral.

By the weekend I was sure that something had happened to Gabi.

Sunday afternoon I called the police and a sergeant took her name and a description in a coldly matter-of-fact way. When I asked him what else I should do he said to just ask around the neighborhood, that her friends should know something.

Chanelle called in the evening and asked me when I was going back. I told her I was going to try Tuesday night but that I had a problem. I told her Gabi's mother had died and we hadn't been able to find Gabi.

"Are you mad at me for what happened the other day?" she asked.

"No, of course not," I said.

"I just wondered why you hadn't called."

"It's this thing with Gabi and her mother," I said.

"Oh," Chanelle said. "I understand. I guess you'll be busy for New Year's?"

Rafe called Monday and asked if I had heard from Gabi, and I told him I hadn't. He said that their grandfather wanted to be sure I would come to the funeral on Tuesday. I said I would be there. I didn't say that my stomach tightened up when I thought about going, or that there was no way I wanted to go if Gabi hadn't shown up. I asked Rafe again if he knew of any places that Gabi could be, and he said no. I called him a jerk for not knowing, and he surprised me by saying he knew he was, but that none of his friends had seen her.

I had been to all the places I had once shared with Gabi, and hadn't found her at any of them. I knew, if she wasn't ill or injured somewhere, that facing her mother's funeral would be hard for her, but facing herself if she didn't go might be even more difficult. Gabi was in trouble, and if I was going to help her, it had to be soon.

I've always believed in barbershops. The one I found in Gabi's neighborhood had framed newspaper photos of boxers on one wall and basketball players on the other. It was two o'clock when I went in, trying to frame the right combination of words. There was one man in a barber's jacket sitting in one of the chairs, reading a paper, and two older men playing checkers.

"Hey, you got here just before the line got long." The barber looked up from his paper and started folding it. "You even get your choice of seats."

"I've got a problem," I said. "I'm looking for my sister. She hasn't been home for three days and we're really worried about her."

"You been to the po-lice?" one of the checker players asked.

"I have, but they don't know anything. Look, she uses drugs, so I think she might be in some place where drug people hang out."

"Then you need to let her stay there," the other checker player said. "Because nothing you're going to tell her is going to get her away from those drugs. And that's what God loves, the truth!"

"Do you know if there are places around here . . . ?"

"Man, you need to get on out of here!" the first checker player said. "We don't use that mess and don't want anybody in here that do!"

I felt incredibly stupid as I turned and started for the door.

"Hey, how much money you got in your wallet?" the barber asked.

"You need to get him on out of here, Frank." The first checker player looked up. "Those people attract trouble like shit attracts flies."

"How much money you got in your wallet?"

I looked in my wallet and came up with twenty-six dollars, all money my father had given me.

"Just a minute," the barber said. "He ain't no junkie. If he was he'd be out here buying dope. Didn't Sister Scott say something about there being a dope place on 121st Street?"

"Yeah, she did," the first checker player said. "She said they go in and out of one of them buildings. But if he ain't buying no dope they liable to kill his skinny butt and eat him. That's the caliber of people you got using that stuff."

The barber went to the phone, looked up a number among all the numbers scribbled on the wall next to it, and dialed it. I heard him say hello to a Sister Scott, ask her if the hot towels had done anything for the pain in her knee, and then ask her what was the number of that dope house she was talking about. He talked to her a little longer before hanging up. He tore off a piece of his newspaper, wrote something down on it, and handed it to me.

"Like Smitty over here said, you messing with dope people you taking your life in your hands," the barber said. "That's the number she give me and it's a basement apartment. If you get yourself messed up don't come crying to me."

"Thanks a lot," I said, taking the paper.

"Don't thank him yet," the first checker player said. "You ain't got your sister, and you ain't come out alive."

The address on 121st Street was less than a block away and I hurried to it. It was an abandoned building. The windows were covered by boards, and there was junk strewn in the well of the basement apartment. A woman sat on the stoop next to it. She was reasonably pretty but blade thin and I figured her for a user. I tried to act casual as I sat down next to her.

"What you want, honey?" Her voice was low, raspy.

"I'm looking for a girl named Gabi. You don't know her, do you? Pretty, dark eyes, light skin?"

"They don't pay me to be seeing people," she said. "You got two dollars you can let me have?"

I didn't answer.

"You looking for a good time?"

Not from you, I thought. "I'm looking for this girl," I said. "And I think she might be inside."

"Give me two dollars and I'll go find out for you." She nudged my knee with her own. "I'm Monica, everybody in there knows me."

I gave her the two dollars.

"I need four."

"You can get it," I said. "But I need to know if she's in there."

"I need it now," Monica said, her voice hardening.

I stretched my legs in front of me and crossed them at the ankles without answering her. She started talking to me again, telling me how she really needed the money, and I looked the other way.

"Why you looking for her?"

"Why? Because she's — Look, do I have to give you my résumé or will you settle for the two dollars?"

"Don't be nasty, baby. Life ain't that long we gotta be taking crap from anybody who come along."

I felt so tired. I could hardly hold up my head. "Look, Monica, I was away at school, and when I got home my girl was using. She says she's just skin surfing —"

"Skin surfing, smoking, whatever, it's all the same."

"Yeah, well, I still love her and —"

"And you don't know what the hell to do."

"And I don't know what the hell to do."

"Did her mama die or something like that?"

"Yeah." I caught my breath. "You know her?"

"Come on with me," she said, taking my hand.

My heart was pumping furiously and my mouth went dry. I didn't want to go with her into the house, and almost pulled away. She rang the bell, two short rings and two long ones. The door opened and beyond it was a wrought-iron gate and behind the gate a face, half concealed in the shadows, its features indistinct. He looked us over quickly, hardly more than a glance, then pulled the gate aside.

The only lights were dim and red in holders along the

walls. I could see bodies lounging around on chairs, some asleep. There was some activity in a corner. A young boy, I figured he was a sticker, was examining the arm of an older man. I looked away quickly. The sound of slow blues came from somewhere. The room was filled with people and yet, somehow, seemed almost to be one huge being. I imagined I could hear its breath, as if some massive creature was crouched in the darkness. The sickening smell of pot filled the air like the smell of fresh blood in a slaughterhouse.

"What's your girl's name?" Monica whispered.

"Gabi," I whispered back. "She's Dominican."

Monica stepped away from my side as she looked around the room. I opened my mouth to suck in what air I could and prayed I wouldn't pass out.

"What you want?" A big dude came up to us. He was in overalls, the kind with the big pocket on the chest.

"Two rocks," Monica said. "Give the man the ten dollars, honey."

Crap. I was too scared to even look at the guy as I took out my wallet, found the twenty, and handed it over. He reached into one of his side pockets, pulled out a bag, and shook the rocks into Monica's hand.

"Where that girl was talking about her mama died?" Monica asked.

The big dude pointed to a dark corner. Monica took my wrist and led me to the corner. In the chair, sleeping with her legs folded under her, was Gabi.

THE BEAST

Gabi opened her eyes and murmured my name. I pulled her upright and she leaned against me, lightly holding my arm. The big dude who had sold Monica the rocks came over and stood menacingly nearby. With one hand around Gabi's waist, I started to leave. He tried to move Gabi's hair away from her face to see what she looked like, and Monica pushed his hand away hard. I kept moving as I felt the small woman's other hand urging me toward the door.

Gabi was unsteady as we hit the street. A light breeze blew bits of colored paper along the sidewalk and the low rumble of distant thunder echoed between the once elegant brownstones. Halfway down the block Monica pointed toward a stoop and said to sit Gabi down for a minute.

"Let's check her pulse," she said.

Gabi was taking deep breaths and tried to put her head down, but Monica pushed her upright and took her wrist. She felt for her pulse, waited a moment, and then said she was all right.

"I don't know what she was using, but if it was blow sometimes they get a fast heartbeat and you have to be careful," Monica said. "Her heartbeat's normal. Give her a minute and she'll be okay."

I looked around and no one seemed to notice us. I thought it would be good to get Gabi off the street, but I didn't want to take her home looking high. I took off my jacket and put it around Gabi's shoulders and she leaned against me. Monica sat next to Gabi and nervously scratched the backs of her hands. It was growing colder and Monica pulled the drawstring on the hooded sweatshirt she wore.

"Yo, Monica, nice looking out," I said. It sounded lame.

Monica looked away and I could see her profile against the changing blur of nighttime traffic. She couldn't have been more than sixteen or seventeen. She noticed me watching her and smiled. Nice smile.

"You ain't never been in no mess like this before, have you?" she asked. "Head joints, people selling dope right out in the open?"

"I've seen some of it," I said. "Never been this close before."

"Ain't nothing pretty about it, that's for sure. And if you stay in it long you won't be pretty, either."

Her lips firmed. For a moment her eyes seemed to tear, and then they were suddenly dry, as if she had, for the moment, willed away the pain.

"How did you . . . ?" I searched for words.

"Get caught up in this mess?"

"Yeah."

"I don't know. It was like, one moment I was walking down the street thinking I was real, thinking I was part of life, and the next moment I wasn't part of it. I was walking and breathing but life had just slipped on away from me. I looked around to see what was happening and I knew it sure wasn't me," Monica said. "And when I fell into the shadows I sure didn't have nobody come looking for me. I don't know if it would have helped if they had."

"Yeah, but drugs are like killing yourself," I said.

"No, it ain't, baby. If you kill yourself you ain't around to say you did it." Monica looked directly at me. "You can use this stuff and make believe you still alive."

"Make believe?"

"Hey, honey, how you doing?" Monica looked past me to Gabi.

"I'm okay," Gabi answered.

"Take her on home and let her get some sleep." Monica stood. "You got cab fare?"

"It's only a block and a half," I said. "We can walk it."

"Stay sweet, baby." Monica touched me on the shoulder, turned, and started down the street.

"Monica. Thanks!" I called after her.

As we started to her house Gabi seemed subdued but alert. At the corner I stopped again and told her that I thought her aunt might be at her house.

She nodded, and kissed me on the cheek. "I'm so wrong," she said, and the tears in her dark eyes spilled over onto her face.

"You walk as strong as you can, and we'll get you home and deal with whatever we have to," I said. "Can you do that?"

She sucked in more air and took my arm.

At the house I rang the bell, and there was no answer. Gabi went through her pockets, found her keys, and gave them to me.

We got upstairs and went in. There was a note on the kitchen table. I picked it up. It was in Spanish and I gave it to Gabi.

"They're going to sit at my aunt's house for the night," she said, after reading it. "They're telling me where the funeral will be."

Gabi sat at the end of the table, put her hands in her lap, and began to cry. I watched as her whole body shook. Looking around, I found some instant coffee and put on the kettle.

"I can't even go to the funeral tomorrow," Gabi said. "I don't have one decent dress. Not one decent . . ."

Tears again. Sobs that filled the small kitchen space, that slowed the hands of the clock on the wall, that framed the pans and dishes on the drain board.

The radio alarm suddenly came on, startling both of us. I looked at the clock, saw that it was nine, and turned off the radio. I made coffee and put a cup in front of Gabi.

"You want to talk to me, Gabi? We've always had good things to say to each other."

Silence. And then me again, pulling a chair next to her,

127

sitting close and touching her hair. "Gabi, please talk to me. Please try."

"I don't have any excuses," she said, her voice trailing off. "I'm just so wrong. I know everything, but still I went the wrong way."

"I'm not asking you to be right," I said. "I'm just trying to understand this thing. Remember when I broke my toe that time, and you and my mother took me to the emergency room?"

"Your mother doesn't like me," she said.

"She likes you, Gabi. Enough to think that I would want to run off with you and not go to college. She just didn't understand you asking me to tell you about the pain, about how much I was hurting. I understood it, and it helped. It helped to search for the words, to bring it into some kind of perspective."

The phone rang. Gabi closed her eyes and picked it up. She spoke in Spanish, and I sensed she was explaining to somebody else where she had been.

"I'll stay here tonight," she said, in English. "I'll see you tomorrow."

She was crying again even before the receiver hit the cradle. "I don't even know somebody to borrow a dress from," she said.

"I'll get you a dress," I said.

"I don't want you to —"

I put my finger on her lips. I knew she had to go to her mother's funeral. I went through my pockets until I found Chanelle's number. I called her and told her I had to borrow a dress for a funeral. She asked me if it was for "my friend," and I said yes.

"What size?" I repeated Chanelle's question to Gabi.

Gabi signaled no, that she didn't want to borrow a dress.

I put my hand over the phone. "For me? Gabi, will you do it for me?"

She told me she wore a size six and I relayed it to Chanelle, as well as the address and how to ring the down-stairs bell. Chanelle said she would try to find something.

I tasted the coffee. It was bitter and weak.

"Do you want to lie down or something?"

"Are you going home?"

"No."

The low hum of the refrigerator shut off and I realized I was hungry. I looked in and saw that someone had brought donuts. I took them out and put them on the table in front of Gabi.

"When you were getting ready to leave I was so happy for you," she began. "I went around thinking of wonderful things to write to you. I was going to invent poetry that you would read and be so glad about me, and about my letters.

"After you left things started falling apart. I kept starting letters and throwing them away. The words wouldn't come, and after a while I knew they wouldn't. You were thinking about me like some kind of amazing poet and that's what I wanted to be. But I wasn't an amazing poet or amazing anything. I'm not. Sometimes I would copy poems from books and string them together in letters. But I couldn't mail them to you. It would be a lie. Like the way you think about me is a lie."

"You're not a lie, Gabi." I took her hands in mine. "You're real and you're here and I do love you."

"That's funny, because I don't love me anymore."

She began to cry again. Softly at first, and then — no louder — but so much harder. So much harder. I felt so helpless. Gabi was hurting and I was sitting right next to her, and I still couldn't reach her pain.

"When Mami found out I was using she got worse. She would stand at the foot of my bed, screaming at me. 'You are a Dominican woman!' she yelled at me. You should have seen her face. Twisted and angry. 'Dominican women don't do this filth!' "

"I'm sorry."

"Then one day everything got to be too much for me. It was too hard to comb my hair. Too far to travel to get to school. Any book I picked up was too heavy. The words were drifting away from me. I could read them, but they had lost their meaning. How can you read words and not know the meaning? How can you walk down a street you've been down a hundred times and not know where it's going, just stumble along until you are lost? Sometimes I thought about being a different person, of going away from you, or you going away from me. I even dreamed of you killing yourself because I had left you."

"I remember the story you told me about Gabriela Mistral," I said. "How her lover had killed himself when she was young. But that doesn't — am I just too out of it to understand this thing?"

"Understand how I could use drugs?"

"Not living in this neighborhood," I said. "Not with all you know."

"The first time I let myself not think," she said. "I was at a party and some people were smoking and some were shooting up. 'Oh, come on, Gabi, this one time won't hurt you. It's not like you're putting it in a vein or something.' I should have left the party. If you had been there I would have left the party."

"I wish I had been there."

"It's no way your fault, Spoon. I couldn't find my way out of my life, and so I just tried to get out of the moment. Every time after that I swore I was going to quit and that I just wanted to get through this one day, this one hour even. I knew you would be disgusted with me. I'm disgusted with me. You know it makes me sick every time? I puke my guts out and then I hate myself even more than before I use the drugs."

"Are you addicted?"

"I don't know the chemistry," she said. "What I know is that I can't let go of the explanation for my life."

"Which is what?"

"Which is the drugs. Can you believe that I feel better thinking that I can't help myself than saying that I just stopped loving myself?"

"The drugs aren't an answer," I said, hating the simplicity of the statement.

"I know," she said. A sparrow's voice. A twig snapping beneath the foot of God. "I didn't ever believe they were."

She asked me for a glass of water from the refrigerator and I got it for her and watched her drink it down quickly. She rubbed the cold, empty glass against her forehead.

"Do you need some sleep?" I asked.

She murmured no, but laid her head down on the kitchen table. I thought about trying to get her to the bed, but I wasn't sure if that was the right thing to do. I remembered movies of people keeping drugged people awake.

I thought of Monica. Of her sitting on the stoop with us, and checking Gabi's pulse. I wondered if she liked herself. People who were kind, I thought, and Monica had been kind to us, liked themselves, or at least wanted to like themselves.

"So what are we going to do?" I asked. "That's what it comes down to, Gabi. What are we going to do?"

"That sounds so hard," she answered. She had her eyes closed and her head resting on her hand.

"How are you feeling?"

"I'm okay," she said. "I'm just so tired. But I need talk. Can you talk to me awhile?"

Gabi's breathing was slow and I thought she was falling asleep. I really didn't know what to say, what to think, or even what I understood.

"Now that I'm home I feel like everything has kind of shifted," I said. "There was a time when the older guys were just hanging around, just drifting through life. It was always the older guys getting into trouble, or the older girls getting into trouble. Now it's my friends — guys like Brian and Leon and Scott — they seem as if they're wandering around in some monster maze. And they're all so cautious, as if any moment they'll either be out in the clear again or something will catch them in the darkness."

"You'll get it all straight," Gabi said, running her hand through her hair. "I believe in you."

I went to the refrigerator and looked for something besides the donuts. There was a pot and I looked in it and saw peas and carrots. I took it out, decided it would be too much trouble to heat them up, and put them back. I was wondering if I had enough money to go out and buy Chinese food when the doorbell rang.

I pushed the buzzer near the door and waited. I thought it would be Rafe or someone else from Gabi's family. It was Chanelle. She stood in Gabi's door, her eyes wide and looking around the apartment.

Gabi stiffened when she saw Chanelle step into the apartment with the shopping bag. I made a brief introduction and Chanelle said she hoped the dress fit.

"I should try it on," Gabi said. She stood as tall as she could; she was much taller than Chanelle as she held the dress up in front of her. "I hope it doesn't fit."

"Gabi!"

"I'm sorry," she said, glancing again at Chanelle. "Let me go wash."

Gabi laid the dress across the back of the chair and went to the bathroom that was just down the hall from the kitchen. I knew she would be crying again.

Chanelle sat at the table and told me that the dress belonged to a girl in her building. She tried not to look around the apartment but couldn't help herself. I wondered what she saw.

We heard water running, and then nothing.

"Do you want me to take it in to her?" Chanelle asked.

"I'll take it," I said.

I took the dress to the bathroom and knocked on the door. There was no answer and an image of Gabi, bending over the sink and bleeding, flickered through my mind. I opened the door.

Gabi, in her bra and underpants, was sitting on the edge of the tub, her head down. Chanelle moved by me and sat next to her. Gabi looked up and managed a small smile.

"I'm just so tired," she said.

I closed the door and went back into the kitchen. I was exhausted, too.

As I waited for them, I thought about all the changes

that had taken place in the few months that I had been away. Clara had gotten pregnant, Scott had dropped out of school, and Gabi, my Gabi, had been using drugs. It was as if so many dreams had suddenly been abandoned, so many lives had been set adrift. I wondered if Monica had once had similar dreams, had once read poetry in the park with someone who had promised her the stars. What were we going to do? I had asked the question of Gabi. What were we going to do? Now that we were glimpsing our whole selves, our selves with blemishes and faults, with saints that sometimes failed us and beasts that sometimes brought us comforts, what were we going to do with these new selves? Could we truly reinvent our dreams? Could we, coupling and tripling with our fellow travelers, find a gentler, easier path to walk upon?

Gabi and Chanelle came out of the bathroom.

"She's beautiful," Chanelle said.

And she was.

ST. JOSEPH'S ROMAN CATHOLIC CHURCH

I n the first row there were five women, a boy, and a blind man. The women were dressed in black, their faces veiled. The man was pale. The yellow streaks in his silver hair reminded me of old newspapers. The boy, Rafe, looked smaller somehow. The suit he wore hung loosely over his thin shoulders. He looked around uncomfortably, as I did, avoiding the dark wooden casket in the front of the church.

Beyond us, beyond the steps and the communion rail and the rows of candles, was the organ. A young black man sat before it, gently touching the keys, almost as if he were trying to awaken them. He was playing from memory, the stiff chords of St. Joseph's intermingled with the soulful monotony of gospel. In this place, at this time, there was a strange mixture of black and Catholic, each claiming the other, each failing.

Gabi was at my side. She was ravishing in black. I was ashamed of my thoughts as she suffered through the funeral liturgy.

Somewhere, in the ordered geography of the church, my parents sat. My father didn't know what to do about me, what to say. He wanted to be understanding, and he was, but his understanding was of another time and, perhaps, of other people. Gabi and I sat apart from the others and I was surprised to find it was me who felt a sense of desperation as I clutched her hand.

The censer swung in a small circle, filling the still air with mist and mystery. It was done with purpose, this putting away, this turning away from life gone stale. There was holy water, a soul refreshed for a final journey.

Gabi leaned against me and her tears burned my eyes.

There were words, the poetry of King James, and they slid through me without touching nerve or sense.

Heavenly Father, bless Lucila and receive her into
Thy kingdom.

Lord have mercy.

Mary, Mother of God, bless Lucila and pray for her.

Lord have mercy.

Gabi knew these words of ancient innocence by heart. How many languages did she know? I didn't know them and my mind, despite my efforts, drifted to the phone call from Chanelle. She was going back to the Academy tonight. What was I going to do?

I did what I understood, but what did I understand? I knew what my father understood, that the Academy was a chance I must take, for which he was willing to make sacrifices. The Academy represented what he wanted for me, a heaven for his Baptist heart. Gabi, leaning forward against the dark pew, was the threat. I imagined him sitting in the living room, his large fingers nervously strumming the arm of the plastic-covered couch, asking me to explain Gabi. How would I arrange the words in my mouth to say that she had simply stopped believing?

I believe in God the Father Almighty, Creator of Heaven and earth, And in Jesus Christ, His only Son, our Lord.

I stood when Gabi stood, and sat when she sat. I learned parts of the Mass. The rituals washed over me and I tried to let them take me away. They moved swiftly along and soon we were filing out of the church into the blinding light of the winter sun. The old man was being led by Gabi's aunt. He walked stoically, a stone man who had learned to grieve within. I imagined tears, like gray pebbles, falling behind his blind eyes.

My parents came to touch Gabi's arm before they returned home. They were sincere and Gabi managed a wan smile. I told them that I was going to the cemetery, and my father said he would see me later.

At the cemetery we waited in cars until the priest was ready, and then we gathered under a small gray canopy. The coffin was already there. It felt as if we were rushing through this last part, as if we needed to get it over with. We said prayers over the grave and over the coffin. We held hands in a moment of silence and then we walked away.

It was late when we returned to Harlem and to Gabi's aunt's house. There was food, wine, and soft drinks. People remembered Lucila, how she had shocked her family by climbing a tree in her Communion dress, how she could sing any song she'd ever heard, how she had always had the prettiest smile of anyone in the family.

Gabi's father. I hadn't noticed him before but then I saw him, sitting on a folding chair, uncomfortable, silent. He joined the conversations by nodding. When people left he looked longingly toward the door. When Gabi went to the kitchen to get me lemonade he went in and spoke to her. Through the door I saw him put his arm around her shoulders. Then he left.

Business. It was decided that Rafe and Gabi would live with one aunt in the Bronx and the old man with another in Harlem. He said he would go back to the Dominican Republic but they didn't take him seriously. How would an old blind man manage? they were thinking. I thought he was already there.

Gabi said she had to go and pulled me out of my seat with her eyes.

"I'll come this weekend to help you pack," an aunt said. She looked at me suspiciously, returned my smile weakly, and turned to Gabi, touching her hair as she spoke. "If you need anything . . ."

The aunt's apartment was on Audubon and Gabi and I took the bus downtown. We didn't talk on the bus or on the walk to her house. Gabi went into the bedroom, took off the dress she had borrowed, and put on a blouse and pleated skirt.

"I'll have it cleaned," she said.

"Give it to me," I said. "I'll get my mom to have it cleaned and send it to Chanelle's house."

"Can you thank her for me? Should I call her?" Gabi asked. "I don't even know her."

"I'll thank her," I said. "How do you feel?"

"A little bit afraid," she said. "I've always been a daughter, 'Lucila's girl with her nose in the air,' my aunt used to say. And now I'm in a new place. But I think that somewhere deep inside I am strong. I am the Dominican woman my mother thought I was. I can do this life, this vagabond road."

"It's going to be hard."

"I know, Spoon, but it's easier when the hard part is in your face. When you don't have choices," she said. "When Mami wanted me to leave school and work and help out with my grandfather I just saw it as the end of my world. I didn't know where to turn. Now, I'll just do the best I can, and maybe it will be enough. Maybe, without her to lean on, it'll be easier somehow."

"I don't know if easy lives here anymore," I said. "I think you reach a point where it doesn't get easier, you just get stronger. I came down from Wallingford looking to find the world I'd left, but it's all changed. You spoke about believing in yourself, and I realize that I've been hearing that question over and over since I've been back."

"I thought you were going to say since you've been back home."

"I am home, Gabi. But home is not what it used to be for me. It used to be simply a neighborhood I played ball in and a building I lived in and where my parents lived. All of a sudden it's a place in which I question everything, mostly who I am. I'm asking myself what does it mean to play ball? What does it mean to sit on the stoop? Can we reach a point where there's just no place else to go?"

"Do you have a different dream when you're at school?"

"I had a different dream," I said. "Wallingford is all about what's going to happen tomorrow, or a thousand tomorrows in the future. It's like when we were kids dreaming about what we wanted to be when we grew up."

"And then one day a really hard "now" awakes us from our nap," Gabi said, putting her hand on mine.

"'And then one day a really hard 'now' awakes us from our nap,'" I repeated.

"What is your 'now'?" Gabi asked. "You got any verbs and adjectives to feed a starving poet?"

"I don't know," I said. "I'm not even sure what there is to know."

It was growing dark. Gabi's half-shadowed face in the dim light reminded me of a woodcut of an angel I had once seen. For a long time we sat in the silence we had drawn around ourselves. Outside the street noises were subdued, only the hissing of tires along the avenue suggesting that life was still pushing relentlessly forward.

"Gabi, I love you," I said.

As the words left my lips the space they vacated was filled with an image by Goya — an aquatint in which soldiers drag women beneath the dark hollow of a bridge. One of the women was Gabi. What did she have to do to get the drugs?

"I love you, too," she said.

"I think, in the end, that matters most," I said.

As the words left my lips the space they vacated was filled with an image by Goya. It is called El Gigante, but it is not of a giant; rather, of a minotaur: half man, half beast. In the corner of the image there is a woman, only half conscious as she lays on a couch. Gabi.

"Gabi, are you going to be okay?"

"Yes, and you have to leave," she said. "You don't have a choice. You have to make these next steps. Finish high school, start college, chase your dreams. It's what I want for you. It's what I want so much for you.

"And I swear to you," she was crying, "I swear with this Dominican woman's brain and with this Catholic heart, that from this moment on I will at least try to be okay."

I went to her and she stood very still and we clung to each other in love and fear.

"If I were a magician I would wave my wand and make everything clear for us," I said.

"If I were a magician I would turn you into a mango and eat you," she laughed. "Then I'd know that I would have you safe inside of me and making me stronger."

It was a nice image. I thought her poetry might be coming back to her. But now it was my throat that felt swollen, my tongue that felt heavy and useless in my mouth. I had to say the words we were avoiding.

"Gabi, how about the drugs?"

She sighed heavily. "I'm not as afraid as I was," she said. "I've been there, if only to visit, and I've seen the beast. There's nothing there that I want. I can't fool myself again."

When I left I was exhausted. My mind drifted through the day, helping Gabi to get ready for her mother's funeral. The church. The singing. But most of all that moment at the cemetery when we had turned away from the coffin, leaving it under the tent for the workers to deal with, when Gabi and I had walked away, neither of us looking back. I felt that I was walking away again, and this time it was Gabi who stayed alone in the darkness. I wanted to think she would be all right, but I didn't know. I didn't know.

I believe in the Holy Ghost, the Holy Catholic Church, the communion of saints . . .

    I believe . . .

RETURN TO WALLINGFORD

The change in Miss Mathews' voice was perceptible. Where it had been warm at our first meetings, now, on the phone in Harlem, it was edged with suspicion. I explained, slowly, carefully, how I understood the seriousness of taking off an extra week. She repeated her feelings of disappointment in me, and said that my lack of an explanation was distressing.

"I can't excuse your absence," she had said. "And I'm sure there won't be much of an opportunity for you to make up the work you'll miss."

She ended the conversation with a good-bye that

sounded forever final, as if she really did not expect me back at all. Maybe she would have had more understanding if I had told her that I would spend the week sitting with Gabi in hospital corridors and rehabilitation centers, searching for one that would take her without health insurance.

The interviews were exhausting and frustrating. We ran into waiting lists, sometimes six months or longer. Sometimes there were special conditions, such as being an expectant mother or assigned by the courts. Sometimes, they were just painful.

"Have you been tested for AIDS?" an older woman, thin, her lips smeared with a bluish shade, spoke loudly as she looked up from her papers.

"I don't have AIDS," Gabi said quietly.

"I didn't ask you if you had it, honey," the woman said. "I asked if you've been tested for it."

"No."

"IV?" the woman asked, certain of her questions.

"I just injected under the skin," Gabi said.

"You used a needle," the woman said, tearing some forms from a pad. "We have outpatient counseling available. Have a seat and fill these out. And this card. Do the card first and give it right back to me. Then a counselor will call you."

The half-filled waiting room was a grimy yellow. There

were couches and a few individual chairs, all green vinyl and chrome, along the windowless walls. Gabi filled out the card with her name and address. There were two boxes, one that said AIDS COUNSELING and the other DRUG COUNSELING. She checked off the drug box and took the card back to the receptionist.

"It's going to take a while." The receptionist raised her voice, making it even uglier than it had been. "You don't have to wait with her if you don't want counseling."

"If you go I'll kill you!" Gabi whispered.

I wanted to go. I wanted to be away from the sordidness of the place, away from the others waiting in the green chairs. A woman, somewhere between twenty-five and ninety, stood and walked across the floor to the magazine rack. Her steps were awkward, stiff-legged, as if there was something wrong with her hips.

"What magazines they got over there?" her companion, a man with heavy shoulders, a beer belly, and spindly legs, asked.

"The usual ones."

"Yeah, okay, bring a couple over."

I kept my head down and followed Gabi's progress as she filled out the questionnaire. How many times married? How many children? Had she been arrested for drug use?

Gabi finished the form and then, with her felt-tip pen, wrote on the palm of her hand *I am crying.*

I kissed her palm, and held her hand, and tried desperately to hold back my own tears. It was a half hour before she was called into one of the offices.

"Hey, man, is she going to intake?" the big man with the spindly legs asked me.

I nodded yes.

"Don't sweat the wait," he went on. "They're slow here and not too many people know about this place. But you come here once a month and they give you your pills for six weeks, which is two weeks better than most of the clinics. You can get three months up near 14th Street but if you got to restart, say, you don't take your pills or your count goes up, they don't switch you to a new regimen right away. That's their problem, they ain't flexible. You know what I mean?"

"Yeah."

"No, you don't know now," he said. "But after a while you'll know."

I knew he was talking about AIDS, not drug counseling. I knew he was welcoming me to the antechamber of the labyrinth. This is what you have to know when you live here, he was saying. This is the language of the beast.

When, fifteen minutes later, Gabi appeared from one of the frosted doors, she was smiling.

"Is it better-looking on the other side of those doors?" I asked.

"No," she said. "But I think I'll come here. I think I'll get along with the counselor. At least she didn't lie to me when I was in there."

I said good-bye to the others as we left. One of the white men called me "brother" and waved a fist at me. Right. Outside Gabi said that she felt as if I were putting her into day care. We laughed. On 8th Street and 6th Avenue we bought frankfurters and orange drinks and wandered into the bookstore across the street.

"Do you think they have a 'Happier Times' section?" Gabi asked.

My parents were upset that I hadn't returned to school. I was upset, too. I had never felt so alone in my life, so unsure of myself. From somewhere an image formed itself in my mind. It was me standing on the stoop in front of my house, with my homeboys — with Junebug and Scott and Brian. We huddled together to comfort one another in the shadows of the tenements.

"No, she's not pregnant," I'd answered my father when he asked.

On the way uptown I asked her if she would really go to the counseling sessions. It was three afternoons a week at first, and later once a week. They did weekly testing, and there was no methadone, so it looked good to me. She said she would. I thought one of the parts of the program, in which people expressed their feelings in journals, would be good for her.

I told my father that I was finally going back to school and he wanted to hire a limo for me. I told him I could manage with the train.

Pennsylvania Station had never been so big as Gabi and I stood waiting for the train to Wallingford. Every time I tried to talk I choked up.

"I want you to be sad to leave me," she said. "One time, when I was young, I saw a snake in a pet shop window. On top of the snake there was a little white mouse. Any moment the mouse knew the snake might eat it. It was shaking and trying to be still at the same time. That's how I feel. I want to believe in myself. I want to believe in myself."

"I am sad," I answered. "Sad and unsure of myself."

"Unsure . . ." She traced a finger from the center of my forehead, down my nose, and onto the center of my lips. " '*Beso que tu boca entregue a mis oídos alcanza.*' 'The kiss your mouth gives another will echo within my ear.' "

"I don't plan to be doing a whole lot of kissing in Wallingford, Connecticut," I said.

"It's almost time for you to go," she said.

"I'll call you," I said. I picked up my bag with one hand and put my other arm around her.

Gabi threw her arms around my waist and clung desperately. "Call me all the time. Write to me."

"I will. I promise," I answered.

We held on to each other on the station platform until we saw the conductor looking down the platform, ready to close the doors.

Gabi looked so small standing by herself, so small and so still, the ever-busy New Yorkers passing in front and behind her until it was only them in a colorless blur as the train plunged into the darkness.

"You going back to school?" The blond man sitting next to me indicated my books with a nod.

"Yes," I said. "I'm a little late getting back, too."

"You kids have it made today," he said. He smelled of aftershave lotion. "If my generation had had the Internet I think we would have done two things: prevented the Vietnam War and solved the civil rights problem a lot sooner."

I was trying to study and wanted to keep my mind on the textbooks, but he had sucked me in.

"How?"

"Okay, first the war." A stubby, well-manicured finger went up. "We could have prevented Nam by actually dropping computers, maybe laptops, right into North Vietnam and giving those people actual lessons on how to farm. That was the major problem there. The Vietnamese were struggling to survive. That's your basic cause for all war. You get a man's belly full, and he won't walk down the street for a war.

"Then the civil rights thing. You realize that most people in America didn't have any idea of what segregation was all about?" The same finger went up. "You saw a few signs, Colored and White, that kind of thing, but most Americans didn't know about what you people were going through until Malcolm X came along. That's when we found out that a lot of blacks hated white people. Your basic liberal, north or south, didn't know that."

He went on, and I closed my book and let my mind wander. I wondered if he knew any black people now, or anything about black life. What would he make of my father? Of Miss Mathews worrying about the black kids without ever mentioning race? What would he have thought of the men in the barbershop or the sister who had spotted the drug house?

I thought of Monica, all skin and bones and heart, pushing her way between the muscle man and Gabi. Could he ever know these people? Could I really know them?

"What's going to revolutionize the Internet," he was saying, "is when they reach a saturation point and realize that they need to charge for people to have Web sites. Then you'll get rid of a lot of frivolous stuff and dead sites . . ."

The truth was that I didn't want him to know about black people, or how we lived in Harlem. These were my people, my parents, my barbershop, my girl, my old lady who sat in the window and looked for crack houses. If he couldn't tell that he was boring me, how could he discover the humanity that seemed so different from the world he knew?

Chanelle had promised to meet me at the Wallingford Station and "tell me the dirt" before I got back to the Academy. I was glad to talk with her on the phone and mildly surprised to hear that I wasn't expected back.

"You know how rumors get started," she had said. "How's she doing?"

"I think she'll make it," I said. "And, Chanelle, thanks for being there."

"Hey!" she said. I had expected more to the sentence, but it hadn't come.

". . . we'll all have devices we wear on our belts to instantly access the Internet wherever we are in the world." The finger was in the air again. "Good grief, are we at New Haven already?"

Downtown New Haven looks better from the train than the streets. My Internet expert began to gather his things and told me to "watch the way the wind blows." I promised that I would.

The conductor announced that the cafe car was closed and there would be a fifteen-minute layover in New Haven. I went out to the platform, found a telephone, and called New York. The phone rang five times as I held my breath.

"Central Intake." The voice sounded vaguely West Indian.

"Gabriela Godoy, please."

"Just a minute."

The on-hold music was B. B. King and I wondered how they had decided he was appropriate at a drug rehab center. I listened to several choruses, then panicked when the operator asked for sixty-five cents more. I fished through my pockets and found two quarters and a dime.

"Please deposit five cents for the next four minutes."

I was desperately looking for another nickel when the

voice came back on. "I'm sorry, she's in a session right now, can you call back in an hour?"

I said I would and hung up. The phone was ringing again, probably the operator looking for her nickel as I got back on the train.

Chanelle was wearing black low-cut jeans and a sloppy green sweatshirt. She smiled as I came over to her and she tried to take my bag.

"I think I can manage it," I said.

The day was unseasonably warm and I didn't have much to carry, so we walked to the campus. The main street in town was trying too hard to be picturesque; the gray, squat buildings down the side street showed the beginning of another season of rainy New England weather.

"You glad to be back?" Chanelle asked.

"Yeah, I am," I said.

"And glad to see your friends?" she asked.

"Delighted to see my friends."

I told Chanelle about Gabi going to the rehab center and voluntarily taking drug counseling. She said she knew a psychiatrist who did drug counseling for show business people, and I thought that was funny.

"Why's that funny?" Chanelle smiled. "That's what he does."

"Maybe it's the way you said it," I answered. "Just one of those things, no big deal."

That bothered her, and she grew quiet. The instant distance made me realize how close we were.

The campus. The tree limbs were still brushed with snow, making them stand out against the black winter sky. The lights that circled the still pond glowed warmly. The pond was still frozen over and a handful of skaters, in twos and threes, glided effortlessly along its surface. But somehow it all seemed less magical now, less inviting. We sat on a bench near the small end of the pond and, in spite of myself, I asked Chanelle what she thought of Harlem.

"I can deal with it," she said. "What did you think of 54th Street?"

"I can deal with it," I said.

"Good." She held out her hand for me to take and, suddenly, I was hesitant.

Chanelle stopped and looked at me, puzzled. I took her hand and held it for a moment against my cheek. And then I kissed her hand, and then I kissed her upturned face as softly, as very softly, as I could.

I was back at Wallingford, away from the landscapes I was only beginning to see with my heart. The journey from the pond to Harlem that I had thought was ended had only begun. At that moment I didn't know what to say to Chanelle, or what to write to Gabi, except that I knew, or was beginning to know, that all journeys are harder than they appear, and that there are often hard roads to climb and beasts to slay along the way.

"Life ain't always simple, is it?" Chanelle said.

"No," I answered. "It ain't."

THE VAN WICKLE GATES, PROVIDENCE, RHODE ISLAND, NINE MONTHS LATER

S mile."

"You bring me to a strange city, put me up against a fence, and then tell me to smile." Gabi has her hand on her hip. "How do I know what you're up to?"

"Try a smile," I say, still looking into the camera. "It won't hurt."

She smiles. A beautiful smile. A radiant smile. A smile that pleases the angels. A smile that pleases me.

I graduated from the Academy over the summer and was accepted at Brown. Gabi had a much harder struggle, graduating but with no scholarships in sight. Then came the realization that Rafe, too, was using drugs. I watched her fight to free herself and her brother from the physical agony and emotional despair of their addiction. It was a draining experience for her. We spent little time together during the summer. She said that she needed to find the strength within herself, that she couldn't lean on me. I remembered what her mother had said, that she was a Dominican woman, and that Dominican women are strong. I didn't know if she would be strong enough, for herself or for Rafe.

At first I didn't know what to do. Twice I walked the streets with her looking for her brother. Once we found him in an empty lot, a needle still in his arm, and sat with him until an ambulance came to take him to the emergency room. It had been a hard summer, a summer of too much pain and too much stumbling through the impossibly mean streets of the city. These were the streets that either sharpened us with their richness and depth or trapped us within endless corridors of desperation.

Gabi had found a job as a stockroom clerk in a bookstore on 12th Street, close enough to the rehab clinic to make all of the meetings. She had stayed with it. I worked on 126th Street at an insurance company and we saw each other some evenings and weekends, but we hadn't been close. She had isolated herself from the world, and from me. I'd understood what she needed to do, how she needed to be strong, to re-examine her life, to recognize the demons that threatened her and Rafe. But I had been put adrift as well. We sat together in the park, or in the library, or in the coffee shops along Columbus Avenue and exchanged small talk, but we had lost the closeness we once had, or perhaps were too cautious to re-explore it. For the first time in my life the streets frightened me. I knew that if Gabi — Gabi with her dark eyes that could stop time, who strung words into casual hymns — if she could lose her way, then so could I.

The summer sped by and soon I was headed to Providence for Brown University's minority students orientation. Gabi had asked me not to make any promises to her, and I had made as many as I could think of. On the morning that I left for Providence my dad picked Gabi up and drove her to work. He parked the car on 10th Street and went to get a newspaper so that Gabi and I could say good-bye.

"He is so old school and corny," she'd said.

"We're supposed to be kissing or something," I answered.

We kissed. We held hands as we walked toward her job. We said good-bye.

I called her from Providence and told her about Brown. In my heart I knew she would have loved it, too. I could sense the disappointment she never mentioned, felt it when she showed up at the railroad station with a slim volume of poetry and a small overnight bag. She had gained some weight and I told her it looked good on her.

"Oh, now you think I'm fat," she said.

"No, I didn't say you were fat," I answered. *Why was I afraid to kid with her?*

We had a tasteless vegetarian lunch in town and I watched Gabi check out all the students around her. I imagined her picturing herself among them.

"They all look so smart and ready," she said.

"Ready for what?"

"For whatever comes their way," she said, staring admiringly at a tall Indian girl in a sari.

She was right. They were ready for whatever came, or at least thought they were. They weren't waiting on street corners, or on stoops, to see what rounded the corners of their lives.

After lunch we walked around the part of town where most of the students hung out. A few spoke to me and I pointed out a couple of others who were in my dorm.

"What are you reading?" she asked.

"Mostly some esoteric stuff that I don't understand," I said. "It looks like everybody here has to bring their own 'I'm smart' flavor to the scene and it has to be different from everybody else's. It's funny."

"It sounds like fun."

"I guess so."

"There are so many different-looking people here," she said. "East Indians, Chinese, a few Middle Easterners. What do you think that guy over there is?"

We are two dancers on a stage, moving without touching, making only the surest steps, not daring leaps.

"I know him, he's from Tibet. You want to meet him?"

"No."

"No problem," I said. I knew these are not Gabi's people. I sensed her discomfort as I touched the straight line of her cheek. "How's Rafe doing?"

"Good," she replied. There was a slight rise in her tone, which made me believe that Rafe was doing well.

"I think that one day we'll put all of last year behind us," I said. "It'll be like some wrong turn that we took."

"I don't think so," Gabi said. "Everything you do becomes part of you. Drugs become part of you even after you leave them behind. They're always there. We don't leave anything behind."

There is an image in my mind, black and white, a dark etching of beasts sleeping in a forest clearing. There is a girl with them. She is awake. What has happened that she will not leave them behind?

We found our way to the Van Wickle Gates and I took pictures of Gabi in front of them. An African student came by and I asked him to photograph us. He took several shots, urging me to put my arm around Gabi, then telling me to put it around her waist when I had chosen her shoulders. Afterward we walked up and down the hills toward the school of design, with me trying to pick out the Brown students from the art students.

"Where is Chanelle going?" Gabi asked.

"UCLA," I said. "She switched schools at the last minute."

"That's a long way," Gabi said. "She'll have to call you."

"She won't *have* to call me," I said.

"She will."

"You jealous of some girl 3,000 miles away?"

"She's not that far away from where you are," Gabi said.

The dancers stop. They measure the distance between them and realize they are supposed to be dancing together. The music slows as they look at each other from across the stage.

"I was thinking how it would be when you came up," I said. "I was imagining you on the train. The first part of the trip was the same as the trip to Wallingford. I was thinking about you looking out of the window and seeing the same things I've seen."

"I was nervous coming up," she said.

"Yeah, so was I. I want things to be good with us."

"It can be good with us without us being, you know . . . having some kind of huge commitment or anything." Gabi tensed her lips, and I wanted to un-tense them with a kiss but was too far away from them. "You'd be a cool best friend."

The music has stopped. I think about Chanelle. About a two-hour phone call from Los Angeles and the two of us recounting the Christmas break in small details as if we had been talking about a movie of someone else's life, as if the Christmas break had been an unfinished documentary. It had been an easy conversation, free of the grainy images of Gabi's apartment or of Harlem Hospital or of the huddled figures on the stoop. It was easy, and seductive. Like sunshine on the pond at Wallingford, like the hot water running off my body in Chanelle's bathroom, like filling in the outlines of pain with the crayon colors of memory, instead of blood.

"I think I don't want to be your best friend," I said. "If what that means is that you won't be part of me any longer." We were passing a coffee shop with outdoor seating, and I pulled her down onto one of the chairs.

"I can't drink any more coffee," she said. "I already have to pee."

I sat down while she went into the coffee house and found the rest room. I could feel my heart beating faster, feel myself becoming nervous. A waitress, buoyant, plump, asked me what I wanted and I stood and said I was just waiting for a friend. She shrugged and went back inside.

I thought about telling Gabi that I really liked Chanelle, but I hadn't allowed myself to love her. I instantly recognized that I hadn't yet thought it all through, and decided not to say anything to Gabi until I had, if ever. What I wanted to remember on this bright day in Providence was how much Gabi meant to me.

She came back from the bathroom and I saw that her eyes were red from crying.

"You okay?" I asked.

"You have to ask me that a lot, don't you?"

"I need to know."

"Are *you* okay?"

"I'm not sure of where we're going," I said. "But I'm

thinking that it's okay not to be sure. I want to be unsure with you, Gabi. I want for you to take a chance being unsure with me."

Gabi swung her head down and away from me. The words had been from my heart, but they hadn't been enough. She needed more.

"Gabi . . ." I reached for her. She turned to me, her smile so sweet, so angelic. My hand was suspended in midair for a long moment, and then she reached for it and took it in her own. She needed a god, and I was only human.

"When I was on the train I played out all these little scenarios between us in my head," Gabi said. We were walking arm in arm, going nowhere in particular. "You were going to beg me for my love and then fall down on your knees, toss a rose over your left shoulder, which would instantly transform itself into an impossibly bright moon, and declare that you are willing to die for the touch of my lips."

"That sounds good," I said, wanting to be the hero of her dreams.

"But you saying that you want to be unsure with me sounds even better, because I know it's from the heart," she said, putting her face against my arm. "I know it's from your heart."

What is from the heart, and what is from the mind? I

didn't know anymore. For a long while we didn't speak. It was almost a relief not to have to find the right words, not to have to measure and weigh how much we both felt. It was turning cool. Leaves danced along the curbs on the evening breeze and the colored pennants outside of the small shops began to flap.

"You know, I have some bad news for you," she said. "It's about Monica."

"What happened?"

"You know I was working with her over the summer and she was really trying to get straight again. I saw her last week and she's way back, man. She saw me and almost ran across the street so I wouldn't see her, but I did."

It was bad news, but worse than the news was that I had expected it, had expected Monica to fail, to go back to the streets, and to whatever she was taking to make her journey easier. I felt sorry for Monica. Grieved for her.

We walked around the campus for another hour, until the early autumn shadows stretched across the cobbled pathways and the summer sun disappeared with an appropriate flourish. Gabi began telling me what she was reading, a new poet published by the Indiana University Press. The excitement rose in her voice as she described the poet's language.

"It's as if she's discovering the simplest words for the first time," she said. "The simplest words, and the simplest emotions, but she brings them alive. Oh, she's simply wonderful."

It was the rich landscape of Gabi's mind that made me want to drop to my knees and throw a rose over my left shoulder, hoping that it would be a moon with enough light to lead us to where we wanted to go.

As she talked, the words rushing from her full lips, we were drawing close again, talking about our dreams. There was the fleeting thought that I might one day lose her again, that now might not ever be forever, that I might never find all the beasts that lay in wait. But I pushed those thoughts aside and told myself to believe in a heart that sees beauty and a soul that prays for love.

We talked until we were exhausted, and then we held one another, and then the day ended with the fat promise of a new one to come.